Weekend at the Ritz

To Tyler
Best Wishes
Frank O'Keeffe

—Weekend at the Ritz —

Frank O'Keeffe

BEACH HOLME PUBLISHERS

Victoria, B.C.

to my children,
Kerry, Kevin and Michael

Copyright © 1993 by Frank O'Keeffe

This edition is published by Beach Holme Publishers Limited, 4252 Commerce Circle, Victoria, B.C. V8Z 4M2, with the assistance of the Canada Council and the B.C. Ministry of Tourism and Culture.

Cover Art: K. Gwen Frank
Cover Design: Michael Dangelmaier, Karo Designs
Editor/Production Editor: Antonia Banyard

Canadian Cataloguing in Publication Data

O'Keeffe, Frank.
        Weekend at the Ritz

        ISBN 0-88878-342-6
        I. Title.
PS8579.K44W4 1993   jC813'.54   C93-091524-0
PZ7.0443We 1993

Also by Frank O'Keeffe:

It's Only a Game

Guppy Love, or, The Day the Fish Tank Exploded

School Stinks!

There's a Cow in my Swimming Pool
(co-authored with Martyn Godfrey)

ONE

If anything is guaranteed to brighten up another boring day at Eastridge High, then Bobby Spezzactena is it. I couldn't see out the bus window because it was all fogged up, but when the door opened I knew from the commotion at the front that we'd reached Spazz's stop.

I yanked off the headphones of my Walkman and quit drumming my fingers on the seat in front of me. Jackhammer's latest hit, 'No Easy Answers' faded to a tinny sound and was then drowned out completely by the hoots of laughter from the kids on the bus. I stared as Spazz made his way down the aisle. Today he was wearing make-up.

"Hi Kevin." He gave me a big grin as he flopped down beside me. Spazz is my best buddy.

I stared at him some more. He had black rings of eyeliner around both eyes. A silver bolt of lightning was etched along one side of his face and disappeared under his shoulder length blonde hair. He had on a greenish cord sports jacket with leather patches on the sleeves that was way too big for him, and a huge purple tie. Spazz bought all his outfits at The Thrift Shop. Somehow the jacket looked vaguely familiar.

"You look crazy," I said. "Okay let me guess. You're the only one who remembered it's Halloween? We're having a parade in home room today and Mr. Dickson is giving a prize for the best costume. You're going as a raccoon, or a panda. Right? I hear pandas are pretty big this year."

Spazz's grin grew wider. He was used to insults.

"No," I continued. "That can't be right. We don't do that any more. We're in tenth grade now. We stopped doing that in grade four. Okay. You haven't slept in weeks because you've been working so hard on that English assignment and that's why you've got black circles under your eyes."

"What English assignment? Have we got one?" Spazz's grin suddenly faded.

"You know. The one that's due today. The twenty questions on that story by Farley Mowat."

"Who?"

"Farley Mowat. You know. The guy who wrote the story about the wolves."

"Oh him. It's due today?"

Even with all that make-up I could see Spazz was worried. Spazz was a headbanger and could answer any question you wanted to know about any heavy metal group, but when it came to English courses he had a real struggle. He tried hard, but it just wasn't his thing. It was funny in a way. He was never embarrassed to dress like one of his favourite rockers, no matter how weird, and he could take all kinds of jibes and insults. But when it came to English class, he really squirmed. I didn't let him suffer long though. He is my best friend. We were just pulling into the school parking lot.

"Naw." I grinned. "It's not due 'till Tuesday. I've got all the notes. We can do it together."

Relief flooded Spazz's face.

"Thanks Kev. You're a life saver."

Before I could stop him, he leaned over and smacked me on the cheek with his lips. It was then I realized he was wearing lipstick.

"Knock it off," I yelled.

That had the effect of drawing more stares and a howl of laughter from the kids on the bus as I attempted to wipe off the lipstick imprint with the sleeve of my T-shirt. God knows what the little kids would tell their mothers when they got home. I could imagine the principal, Mr. Norton, getting phone calls from mothers, worried about the perverts on their son's or daughter's bus. Sometimes having a friend like Spazz can be a problem.

"Bring your notes with you," Spazz said. "We're gonna have to skip out just after English anyway. There's been a slight change of plan. We've gotta be downtown at noon."

"What? What's going on? I thought you said we were starting this job tomorrow morning. You didn't say anything about skipping classes."

I followed Spazz off the bus and steered him into the nearest washroom. I was thankful it was deserted except for the usual cloud of cigarette smoke.

"Okay, so tell me what we're doing? You did say it was legal." I checked my face in the mirror. I'd got most of the lipstick off and there was just a bit of a smear on my cheek. I washed it off.

"It's legal. And you're gonna get the two hundred and fifty bucks like I said. And you won't be needing this." He tossed my bag lunch into the trash can.

"Hey," I protested. "I made those sandwiches myself."

"You can't go walking into where we're going carrying a bag of bologna sandwiches. It doesn't look good. Anyway, we're having lunch there."

"They weren't bologna, they were ham and cheese. And what's this about having lunch? You buying? Come on, I've been waiting all week to find out what we're doing. I told my mom we had a job for the weekend, and when she asked what it was, I was so vague, I think she suspects we're gonna rob a bank or something."

The bell rang for the first period class.

"Relax, Everything's cool. I told you I'd explain everything at the right time. You'll know by noon today, and it's legit. The only illegal thing we're doin' is skipping school after second period and that's not exactly a hanging offence."

We went to our lockers and Spazz got one or two stares from kids in the hall but most of them were used to him by now.

He was chattering on about Black Vulture's latest release, but I found it hard to concentrate. In the back of my mind it clicked that Spazz was made up like Black Vulture's lead singer except his shoulder length hair should've been black instead of blonde. I was still worried about all the secrecy. Spazz had only told me he had a job for the weekend that would pay a lot of money and that my cut was $250. Although I'd bugged him every day to tell me more, he'd refused. "Sworn to secrecy," he'd said and, "where can you get two hundred and fifty bucks for two days work where you don't have to work up a sweat, and accommodation and food is thrown in?"

It was the two hundred and fifty bucks that got me hooked. At best I could make fifty bucks on a weekend in the summer mowing lawns if I worked like a dog. This was winter and I was flat broke.

Another reason I wasn't concentrating on what Spazz was saying was because Debbie Dobrazynski had just walked past and was getting her books from her locker. Debbie was every tenth grade guy's dream and probably all the guys in grades nine, eleven and twelve as well. She never noticed me though. She noticed Spazz alright. Everybody notices Spazz. An amused grin spread over her face. She had a great smile and I tried to catch her eye but she looked right through me, and then went back to getting her stuff out of her locker.

I closed my locker, spun the combination and Spazz and I headed for class.

"Hey guys, wait up." Lauren Malone caught up with us. "My God, Spazz. You really look radical today. Who are you this time?"

"He's Black Vulture with blonde hair," I said,

"I thought maybe a penguin." Lauren laughed. "Really Spazz. You're just too much. Dickson will have a convulsion when he sees you. I guess Black Vulture's concert was really great, huh?" Lauren glanced at me quickly and I blushed.

"The greatest," Spazz said.

Lauren is a really nice kid. I like her. She's no Debbie Dobrazynski but she's pretty cute all the same. I'd taken her out a couple of times, but nothing heavy, if you know what I mean. It had been nearly two weeks since our last date and that had been a bit of a disaster to say the least.

I was supposed to get tickets for Black Vulture's concert. The day the tickets went on sale I was to meet Spazz at dawn outside the Palladium. I'd slept in and the tickets sold out. Spazz could easily have bought the tickets because he was first in line but when I didn't show, he thought I'd changed my mind. I'm not as big a fan of Black Vulture as Spazz is, but, as I found out when I took Lauren to a movie instead, Black Vulture is her favourite group. She'd had her heart set on going to the concert and when I didn't come up with the tickets, she was really disappointed. She said she would have got them herself.

To make matters worse, I'd told her the movie would be great, but it turned out to be a dud. I knew she was mad when she wouldn't let me kiss her goodnight but just said, "Thanks for the movie Kevin," and stomped into her house.

Mr. Dickson, our home room and Social

Studies teacher, did a double take when Spazz walked into the classroom, but he recovered quickly.

"And who have we here? No don't tell me. Let me guess. Ah, I can't be fooled that easily. Yes, it's Bobby Spezzactena. Too bad the plastic surgery didn't work, Bobby. I think I'd ask for a refund. I like the jacket though. It makes a nice contrast with the tie."

The class laughed and Spazz laughed along with them. Mr. Dickson wasn't such a bad guy.

We slipped out the east door of the school just before third period and headed over to Broxton Street. Broxton is the main drag in our neighbourhood.

I was fumbling in my pocket for exact change for the bus fare when Spazz hailed a cab. My mouth dropped open and I was about to tell him that I didn't have much money, but Spazz waved off my protest.

"It's on me. I got an advance." My mouth dropped even further when we got in the cab and I heard him say, "Take us to The Ritz Plaza." The Ritz Plaza is the classiest hotel in the city. If my bag lunch would have been out of place there, what about Spazz? I couldn't help wondering, whatever the job was, how would Spazz get past the front door looking like he did?

TWO

"And keep the change."

"Thanks buddy. Have a nice day."

I gulped. Spazz had just given the cab driver a ten-dollar tip. Spazz — my best friend who had to borrow fifty cents from me last week to pay for his cheeseburger in Burger King. But I hadn't time to think about that. The door of the cab was being held open by The Ritz Plaza's red uniformed doorman and it was his turn to gulp when Spazz stepped out.

Spazz walked up the red carpeted steps to the plate glass doors of the hotel like he owned the place. I followed, expecting to be tossed off the steps at any minute. Spazz paused on the top step and the doorman scurried up after us.

He looked uncertain about opening the door. His face had turned as red as his uniform. Spazz slipped a five dollar bill into the hand of the doorman, who instantly got over his embarrassment. With a tip of his gold braided hat, he murmured, "Thank you sir," and we were through the doors into the plush carpeted lobby of The Ritz.

The baby blue carpet was so soft and thick, I thought, this is what it must be like to walk in those white fluffy summer clouds. I was ankle deep in the stuff. I was glad, because I thought maybe my grubby sneakers wouldn't be so noticeable.

I stared around the lobby. I'd never seen anything like it except in the movies. It was huge and so luxurious you'd have to earn a mint to even dream of checking into a place like The Ritz. No wonder Spazz had forked out five bucks just to get us inside the door.

Around the edges of the carpet stood tenfoot-high potted palms. A chandelier that must have weighed a couple of tons hung from the ceiling and twinkled and sparkled like a million ice crystals. A huge check-in counter with a brass plated front was off to our right. The brass was so highly polished I could see my reflection, except it was a bit like looking at myself in one of those crazy mirrors they have in fun fairs. A number of guys in gold embroidered shirts, gold-striped black pants and little pillbox hats were clustered around the counter, helping with luggage and escorting people to and from the elevators nearby. I figured they must be bell hops.

A couple of other guys wearing dark blue turbans, pale blue high-collared jackets, white baggy pants tucked into long white socks and weird pointy slippers turned up at the toes, were also standing around. I couldn't guess what they were. Maybe they were guests from some exotic country. They looked like they had a magic carpet tucked behind one of the potted palms. It was just like a fancy dress party or something from the Arabian Nights. Everyone was in costume. I felt conspicuous in my jeans and black T-shirt with a red number 14 on the back. Spazz's Thrift Shop jacket looked even more thrift-shoppy in this place.

Soft classical music filled the air and I gasped when I saw what I thought was a full size orchestra on our left. The clink of glasses and silverware told me that the people sitting at tables were having lunch and the orchestra was entertaining them. The tables were covered with gleaming white tablecloths and each table had a huge bouquet of flowers. Waiters, who looked like penguins, in tuxedos and starched white shirts, scurried about talking in whispers, delivering food, pouring wine and taking orders.

"We're gonna have lunch here?" I whispered to Spazz.

"Ahem. May I help you?" Another penguin-like figure who looked like the king penguin, blocked our way. He was totally bald and wore a red cumberbund around his bulky waist. He had a small gold name tag in his lapel that said Maitre D'. I wondered what the D apostrophe stood for. Maybe he was half French and half Irish or something. But whatever he was, I knew he spelled trouble. His frown and the way his nose tilted told me we had about five seconds to get back out onto the street before some of his goons appeared from behind the potted palms and turfed us out.

"Ah yes," Spazz said. He fished in the top pocket of his jacket, produced a small card and handed it to Baldy.

Baldy peered at it suspiciously like he'd just been handed a used Kleenex, then, like a light coming on, he suddenly beamed.

"Welcome to The Ritz, gentlemen."

He wheeled around, snapped his fingers and out of nowhere one of those magic carpet guys appeared.

"Ah Stanley. Show these gentlemen to the Royal Suite."

Stanley! I was sure his name would be Abdul or Aladdin or something, but no, sure enough, his name tag read Stanley. I wondered if his toes curled up inside his weird slippers.

Stanley nodded politely. "This way gentlemen." He set off towards the elevators to the left of the check-in counter and we hurried after him.

I couldn't believe what was happening. What was on the card that Spazz had shown to Baldy? And what was the Royal Suite?

Up close, Stanley looked like any ordinary guy from Eastridge High, except for his costume that is.

"What's your job here, Stanley?" I couldn't resist asking.

He smiled as he produced a key from his pocket, opened a small box on the wall of the elevator and pressed a button inside.

"I'm with customer relations," he said.

The elevator doors closed and we began to rise. I hadn't a clue what customer relations meant, but Spazz filled me in.

"He means he's with security," he said.

Stanley continued to smile, but said nothing.

I wanted to ask Spazz if the job we'd got meant we'd have to wear a crazy outfit like Stanley's but, if it is a security job, I thought, I'd better keep my mouth shut, like Stanley. I couldn't see myself chasing down any criminal types wearing a pair of curled up slippers. I studied the numbers as they lit up above the door. We reached 34 and I expected we'd stop. There weren't any higher numbers, but the elevator continued on, I guessed, for about two more floors. The doors slid back and Stanley stepped out and kept the doors from closing again.

"Gentlemen." He waved us into a carpeted hallway and his smile widened as Spazz slipped him some bills. He gave a quick bow and disappeared into the elevator. I could see how we'd make a lot of money here, especially if all the patrons of The Ritz handed out money like Spazz.

I was about to say something when I realized there was a guy sitting at a desk across the hall — if this was the boss, or we were going to be interviewed, I wished Spazz had warned me. I would have put on a better shirt and pants.

"Gentlemen." The guy wore a dark suit and tie and he didn't smile. He looked kind of hard nosed. "May I see some identification?"

Identification. What could I show this guy. I didn't have a driver's licence or credit card or anything. I think the only thing in my wallet with my name on it was my Blockbuster Video Store card and I doubted if it would be good enough. But I shouldn't have worried. Spazz produced his magic card again and the guy at the desk seemed to relax. At the same time a door behind the desk opened and a young guy with long black hair and a droopy moustache beckoned us in. He looked vaguely familiar. "It's okay," he said. "We're expecting them."

Who is? I wondered.

We stepped around the desk and into the room.

If I thought the lobby was out of this world, then the room we stepped into beat it hands down. The carpet was even thicker here and the view from the huge windows was fantastic. The room itself was twice as big as my house and the furniture looked like it had just come out of a showroom. I got a quick glance at a well stocked bar and a stereo system that covered one wall before I noticed a figure rising from a plush armchair, his hand outstretched.

"Welcome Bobby. Good to see ya. Glad you could come a day early. As I told you on the phone, there's been a slight change of plan." He shook Spazz's hand then reached for mine. "This must be Kevin."

"Hi," I croaked. My voice sounded strangled.

I was shaking hands with Billy T Banko. *The* Billy T Banko, lead singer of Black Vulture, the biggest heavy metal sensation of the whole rock scene. Their latest album had gone platinum in a matter of weeks and Rolling Stone called Black Vulture 'The Band of the Decade.'

"And this is Mike Helitizer, my drummer. Mike is gonna be our best man."

Mike waved. "Hi."

What's going on? All sorts of crazy thoughts were racing through my mind. It sounded like Billy T was getting married, but what had Spazz got to do with it?

"Okay," Billy said. "We haven't got much time. There's a plane waiting at the airport. We've gotta be there in an hour. First off, Bobby, I want you to wash off that make-up. I only wear it for live performances. Ah, here's Victoria. Vicky, meet Bobby and Kevin. They're gonna cover for us while we're gone."

The woman, who had suddenly appeared from another room in the suite, was stunning. I could only stare. The closest I had ever been to something like her was Debbie Dobrazynski but Debbie was a tenth grade student. Vicky was a woman and I mean woman. Her copper-coloured, shoulder length hair gleamed and her green eyes seemed to smoulder, but the way she moved across the room to Billy T's side was what made me hold my breath. I couldn't figure out how she moved in the dress she was wearing. It seemed to be painted onto her flawless body. Billy caught me staring.

"Cute, huh?" He grinned.

Vicky flashed a wide smile and gave Billy T a peck on the cheek. "Pleased to meet you, Kevin." She took my hand and I could smell her perfume. She turned to Spazz. "Bobby, my ... he does look like you. Maybe I should marry him instead." She laughed and held Spazz's hand and gazed into his face. I saw Spazz blush.

"Okay, Bobby," Billy said, "get the make-up off, the bathroom's back there. You all packed hon?"

Vicky nodded.

Spazz was back a few minutes later minus his black-eyed circles, lightning flash and lipstick.

"Good," Billy said. "Now, let's have your jacket and tie. This afternoon, you and Kevin can take a stroll through a few stores downtown and maybe part of the mall, but make it fast. You don't want to linger too long, some of those groupies will tear you apart to get a piece of you. Just let yourself be seen and get back here quickly. Here, take a look."

Spazz and I followed him to the huge picture window. "See them?" He pointed down the block to the street corner. "That's some of them. They think I'm here." A small group of girls were lounging or sitting against the wall of a building opposite the hotel entrance. "They can be dangerous. Whatever you do, don't bring any of them back here. The hotel will get upset. Security will keep them out. Now, you can order whatever you want from room service, so don't eat out. Here, you'd better practice my signature. We also want the hotel staff to think I'm still here."

Spazz copied Billy's signature a number of times.

"Good. That looks fine. Now make yourselves at home, use the bar, uh, maybe go easy on that, play some tapes, there's a stack of them on the stereo, watch TV, whatever. Okay, put this on."

I blinked when Billy reached up and whipped off his long black hair. Beneath, his hair was brown and cut short and he didn't look like Billy T Banko at all. But Spazz did, the spitting image, once he got the wig on. He had the same curved nose and dark eyes and if I hadn't known it was Spazz, I would have been fooled. "Looks great." Billy adjusted the wig on Spazz's head, making sure Spazz's blonde locks were fully covered. "Remember, don't let the hotel staff see you without this on, and don't let any of those groupies get their hands on you or my cover is blown. You're gonna have to be his baby-sitter, Kevin. Keep him out of trouble. You have to convince everyone that we're still here otherwise our wedding will become a zoo and I want to keep it very, very private. Now for some clothes. You too, Kevin. You don't have to look like a Black Vulture member but one of my roadies will be fine."

I was still reeling from the shock. Spazz was going to make believe he was Billy T, leader of Black Vulture while Billy, Vicky and Mike flew off somewhere for a private wedding and I was to become a Black Vulture roadie.

"Okay you guys, thanks a lot. We're off." Billy, complete with a blonde wig, Spazz's Thrift Shop jacket and purple tie, waved good-bye as he and Mike slipped out the door. Mike was wearing my T-shirt. He had removed a wig too and his moustache had disappeared. Vicky sat and waited. She was going to slip out ten minutes later.

Spazz and I said nothing. We just sat staring at Vicky.

"Relax, boys. Just remember what Billy said and everything will be fine. I really appreciate what you're doing. I couldn't stand a wedding with all those reporters sticking microphones in my face and popping off flash bulbs. Well, it's time. I'm meeting Billy and Mike in a parking lot down the block. Billy has an old car from Rent-A-Wreck stashed there."

She slipped a raincoat over her dress and covered her hair with a headscarf. She put on a pair of dark sunglasses, picked up her purse and headed for the door.

"Bye now," she murmured. "I hope you boys won't be too bored."

"We'll try not to be," Spazz said. "But Kevin did bring notes for English homework."

I suddenly remembered. "I left them in the cab."

"Great." Spazz grinned. "We definitely won't be bored then."

"See you Monday evening," Vicky said.

"Have a great wedding," Spazz called.

All I could think of to say was, "But I have to be home by Monday."

It was too late. The door closed behind her. Spazz looked at me, then let out a whoop. "I'm a Black Vulture. For the whole weekend."

"Yeah. Well right now, I think I'm just chicken," I said.

THREE

"What do you mean, chicken? Look what we've got," Spazz waved his arm around the suite. "Any kid in Eastridge High would give his eye teeth to be in our position. Come on, let me show you around. I got a quick look when I went to the bathroom. You know, it's got three bedrooms, and wait till you see the hot tub. Man, this place must rent for about two grand a night."

I followed Spazz. The beds were all king-size and each room had its own set of furniture, TV, a phone and full size private bathroom.

"Wow," I said. "There's enough towels here to cover the walls."

"Yeah, and look," Spazz pointed. "Bathrobes, all kinds of soap, shampoo, mouthwash, cologne, it's all here."

"Yeah, but how many showers and baths can you take?"

"Come on. I'll show you the main bathroom. As well as the usual bath and stuff, it's got a hot tub, and even a TV. We can soak in the tub tonight and watch our favourite shows, they've even got videos. You want to watch an X-rated one? You just phone down to the front desk and they put one on for you, great huh? Look at this. Here's the list." Spazz grabbed a card off the top of the TV as we crossed the living room. "Hey, Kevin, look at these titles." He rolled his eyes. "Anyway we can decide that later. Here's the master bathroom. It's huge."

He was right. I'd never seen such a huge bathroom. It was gleaming tile after gleaming tile. Right in the middle, a blue, oval-shaped hot tub that could hold at least six people, bubbled quietly.

"Watch this." Spazz pressed a button on the control panel near the edge of the tub. There was a rumble as the jets inside the tub went into action and the water churned. "Great, huh? Come on, I'm hungry. Let's order some food."

He switched off the jets and disappeared into the living room. I found him sitting in an armchair studying a menu. "Spazz. We've gotta talk."

"Yeah?"

"Yeah. What's gonna happen when the guy

outside the door, or Stanley and his pals, realize we're not Black Vulture?"

"Relax. We're only going to go out once and walk around for a while. We'll order all our food from room service. We'll only see whoever delivers the food. And anyway, I do look like Billy T, even Vicky said so. So, if Stanley and his boys see us, it will only be when we do a fast walk through the lobby. Billy T wants us to be seen, remember? Now, you want a steak or what? A New Yorker or a big T-bone, or how about some pizza?"

"Hang on a sec, How did you get this job anyway? You wouldn't tell me anything about it, and now, according to Vicky, we're here till Monday evening. I told my mother we'd be working somewhere all weekend, but we'd be back Sunday night."

"So, phone her up. Tell her the job's gonna take longer than we thought. I don't know why you're worrying so much. We've got a great place to stay, great food, even drinks if we want them, and on top of that we get paid. You're gonna get two hundred and fifty bucks just to keep me company. I'm getting five hundred! But then, I'm in the starring role." Spazz grinned.

"So why you? How come Billy T picked you? Do you know him from somewhere?"

"I do now. Look, you know I went to the Black Vulture concert ten days ago, the one you missed because you were trying to put the moves on Lauren Malone or something? You really should have taken her to the concert instead of that movie. She'd have given her right arm to go to the concert." Spazz laughed. "She might have given you more than her right arm if you hadn't been so dumb. Anyway, I went by myself and I was right up front. Part way through the concert, one of Billy T's roadies comes up to me and says Billy T wants to see me in his dressing room afterwards. I thought he was putting me on."

"Anyway Billy T decided I looked enough like him to offer me the job. But he swore me to secrecy. Said I could bring one other guy, that's you. But I couldn't tell you what we were doing. Billy T figured if I told anyone, all the kids in Eastridge High would want to be in on it and the whole thing would blow right open. The press would swarm this place. Billy T and his band left town right after the concert but he and Mike slipped back in here last night. Vicky comes from here and he came to get her. End of story. Now can we eat? I'm starved."

FOUR

We were eating lunch, although I wasn't quite sure what mine was. Half the stuff on the menu was in French and when Spazz rang for room service I'd simply pointed out my selection on the menu. I guess Spazz's pronunciation wasn't too great or something, but I always thought *à la mode* meant you got ice cream on the side. What I got was some kind of meat covered in a mushroom sauce. I checked the menu again. What I'd got was *Le coeur de filet de boeuf à la mode du patron*. Spazz had a whole lobster and a chocolate soufflé.

When the guy from room service wheeled in the trolley, everything was covered with silver domed lids. Spazz had me give the guy a five-dollar tip.

"How much money did Billy T give you?"

I'd asked. "Is this out of your five hundred?"

"Naw. He gave me a hundred and fifty bucks and told me to use it all up. I guess he's a big tipper and wants to keep up his image."

Spazz wiped his mouth on his linen napkin then dibbled his fingers in a small bowl of water with a slice of lemon in it. "Neat huh? They even give you finger bowls?"

"Finger bowls! I drank mine. I thought it was pretty weak lemonade."

Spazz laughed. "You gotta stop eating at McDonalds. How are you ever gonna get educated?" He got up and looked at himself in a mirror. "It's time for our stroll. You ready?"

"I've just got to brush my teeth. Good thing they supplied toothbrushes."

As I brushed my teeth I heard the stereo come on and I got back to find Spazz prancing on top of one of the coffee tables, making like he was Billy T playing a guitar. Spazz was miming the words of Black Vulture's latest hit as the stereo blasted out the song.

Blondes at the barricades
Keeping me back from you
Blondes at the barricades
Only my dark-haired girl will do
For me
Blondes at the barricades
Blondes at the barr-i-cades,
Holding me back

Under attack
I'm fighting back
Coming to you
Blondes at the barr-i-cades

Spazz noticed me, jumped down from the table and turned off the stereo. "Great, huh? Okay, Let's go."

"Where are we going?"

"Just a couple of blocks, maybe walk through that mall, what's it called, Van something?"

"Van Cruise. It's got some pretty fancy stores."

"Well come on. Let's have some fun. I'm beginning to feel like Billy T already."

I put on the jean jacket that Billy T had given me. It had a small Black Vulture crest on the right shoulder. Spazz wore a white shirt with a high banded collar and a black, waist-length fitted jacket with straps across the shoulders. His pants, also Billy T's, were black and tight fitting. He looked a far cry from The Thrift Shop. We slipped out the door and the guy at the desk outside gave us a quick salute and wrote something down in a small book. The elevator came almost right away and we got in.

"Hey," I said. "How does this work?"

"Just press M for main," Spazz said. "I can understand you not knowing about finger bowls but I thought you'd at least know how to work an elevator."

"No. I mean, how do we get back up? Do we have to get Stanley and his key?"

"Probably. But right now we want to go down. Press M for Pete's sake."

I did. When we reached the lobby I wanted to run to the front door, but Spazz wanted to make the most of his first real test as Billy T. He strolled across the carpet and I saw both Stanley and the Maitre D' guy nod as we passed. Ahead, I saw the doorman trot to the door, ready to open it as soon as we got there. A low murmur came from some of the diners at the edge of the lobby and I heard someone whisper, "It's Billy T. Shssh. He'll hear you. You know. The rock band, Black Buzzard." I thought for a minute that my mother must have been there. She never gets the names of rock bands right. I must remember to phone her, I thought.

"Taxi sir?" It was the doorman.

"No thanks." Spazz said. "We'll walk."

"Very good sir. It's a lovely day for it."

We were out on the street and I wanted to burst out laughing, but Spazz gave me a warning look.

"Keep cool," he said, grinning. "Don't blow it now. We've gotta walk around for a bit and get back inside as Billy T and friend, otherwise it's back to Burger King or McDonalds without the finger bowls."

We walked about a block and then crossed the street. As we crossed, I noticed the small group of girls that Billy T had pointed out were now walking quickly down the sidewalk towards us.

"Don't look now," I said. "But I think we're being followed."

"Great. I see them. They must believe I'm Billy T. We'd better not let them catch up to us right away." Spazz quickened his pace but so did the girls. When we heard squeals and screams behind us, we broke into a jog.

We got to the end of the block and turned the corner. I thought I heard a yell behind us, It sounded like, "I love you Billy."

"Do you think we should let them catch up?" Spazz asked. "A couple of them look pretty cute."

"I think that's a bad idea. Remember what Billy T said about them being dangerous. What if they find out you're just Spazz?"

"Too bad. I've never had girls chase me before." Spazz came to an abrupt stop and ducked into a doorway — I followed.

"Let's go in here and see if we can give them the slip," Spazz said.

"In here?"

"Yeah."

"But it's Friedbergs. You ever been in here?"

"Once. They asked me to leave and I was dressed better than I am now. I think I'll buy a tie. Let's see if they like Billy T's money better than Bobby Spezzactena's."

"You're crazy, Spazz."

"Yeah."

Spazz pushed open the door and we were in the most expensive and exclusive men's store in the city.

"Good afternoon. Are you looking for something in particular?"

We were confronted by a guy with slicked down hair. He was wearing a stiff white shirt with a dark grey tie, grey striped pants and a black coat with tails. A real red carnation was stuck in his lapel. I could smell it.

"Uh. Yeah. Maybe a tie. Something bright," Spazz said.

I was ready to back out the door. The way this guy was looking down his nose at us made me feel like we were something bad that was stuck to the sole of one of his black polished shoes.

"Really gentlemen, I don't think we'd have anything to suit your taste. I …"

"Mr. Banko. What a pleasure to see you. It's been such a long time since you've visited our establishment." Another tailored dummy rushed forward and shook Spazz by the hand. "I'll take care of Mr. Banko and his friend, James."

"Very good, Mr. Charles." James gave a curt nod and seemed to merge into a rack of grey suits.

"You must forgive James. I don't think he recognized you, Mr. Banko. I don't think he was here on your last visit. Now, how can I be of assistance?"

"I think I'd like a tie. Something colourful. Maybe in red," Spazz replied.

"But of course. Just step this way. Let me show you some of our latest creations from Paris. Pure silk, hand painted. This way."

Spazz and I followed Mr. Charles to a corner of the store where hundreds of ties hung on racks or were spread fan-like in frames, like paintings, along the walls. Mr. Charles waved them all aside and opened the drawer of a large chest. "Ah, here they are. These are exclusive to Friedbergs. Exquisite, yes?"

Spazz and I peered into the black velvet-lined drawer. About a dozen ties in various red shades were pinned neatly to the velvet. The designs were really something. Sea horses, shells, miniature flowers, tropical plants and other designs covered the ties.

"I like this one." Spazz pointed to a pinkish red one with mermaids neatly drawn in black.

"An excellent choice, Mr. Banko, and perhaps something for your friend?"

"Uh. No thanks," I said.

"Come on," Spazz said. "It's on me."

"Well I..." On him? I thought. We didn't even know how much these ties cost. This wasn't The Thrift Shop, this was Friedbergs.

Mr. Charles beamed and pulled open another drawer. "Perhaps something in blue?"

"Hey! Those look neat," Spazz said.

I stared into the drawer. A dark blue tie with tiny yellow butterflies caught my eye. "That looks fantastic," I said. I thought, I wonder what Lauren Malone would say if I wore that on our next date. That is if there is a next date. "Will there be anything else gentlemen?"

"No, not for today, thanks," Spazz said.

"Shall I put these on your account, Mr. Banko?"

"Um." Spazz paused. "Oh, by the way, uh, how much are they?"

"Ninety dollars plus tax, Mr. Banko."

I stifled a gasp and saw Spazz gulp.

"Um. Okay. Put them on my account."

"Very good sir. I'll just get them wrapped and bring your bill for you to sign, I won't be a moment."

When Mr. Charles hurried away I hissed, "Ninety bucks plus tax for two ties. How can you charge that to Billy T? We'll be charged with fraud if this Mr. Charles guy finds out who you are."

"I didn't know they'd cost that much and I'm not sure I have enough money left. Anyway, relax. Billy T said I could buy a couple of ties to replace the one he got from me. I didn't know he had an account here."

"But yours only cost fifty cents at The Thrift Shop, and you're gonna charge Billy T ninety bucks for a couple of replacements?"

"Actually, I think that's ninety bucks each."

"Each!" I gasped.

"I didn't know they would be so expensive. I was going to pay cash. When Mr. Charles asked if I wanted to charge them to my account, that is, Billy T's — I figured, why not? How would it look if Billy T said he couldn't afford them? I'll straighten it out with him later."

"Well you can take the money out of your share. I didn't want a tie in the first place."

"Here you are, Mr. Banko. If you'll just sign here."

Mr. Charles handed Spazz a bill and he scrawled the best imitation of Billy T's signature that he could, considering his hand was shaking. "And there you are sir, your ties. It's always a pleasure to serve you. Do come again soon. I ... What is it, James? What girls?"

The look on Mr. Charles' face changed from one of puzzlement to one of horror as he stared towards the street. The group of young girls who had been following us had grown larger and some of them were making a mess of Friedbergs' polished windows by pressing their faces against the glass. Some of them seemed to be actually kissing the glass, leaving wet lipstick prints all over it. Another group were pressing against the door, trying to force their way in, while James was doing his best to keep the door closed. The girls seemed to be winning.

"Mr. Banko," Mr. Charles gasped. "I think you've been discovered by some of your, er, fans. I'm afraid you'll have to use the back door. It will let you out onto Van Cruise Mall. I'm sorry about this, sir, but if I don't get you out of here quickly, there's no knowing what damage those ruff … er, young girls might do. This way gentlemen, if you please."

There was a look of panic in Mr. Charles' eyes as he ushered us to the back of the store and through a small office area where he unbolted a door. "Hurry gentlemen, good luck and thank you."

We stepped out into a narrow passageway next to some public washrooms in the mall. Before Mr. Charles closed the door behind us there were screams from inside Friedbergs and the harried voice of James yelling, "Ladies! Please! Control yourselves!"

FIVE

We walked quickly through the mall.

"Hey! Look. There's me."

A larger than life-size cardboard cutout of Billy T, complete with lightning flash on his cheek, stood outside the door of a record store. It was advertising Black Vulture's latest release, *Blondes at the Barricades*. The cardboard Billy T had a cardboard blonde girl clinging to him and the jacket he was wearing looked exactly like the one Spazz had on.

Spazz stood beside it and struck a pose. A few passer-bys stared at him.

"Come on, Spazz." I grabbed his arm and pulled him along the mall. "You look too much like that cardboard dummy. We'll get mobbed."

"I wouldn't mind getting mobbed by a

blonde like that." Spazz grinned.

"Come on," I said. "Billy T wanted you to just put in an appearance, not cause a riot."

"There can't be any harm in talking to a couple of girls."

"I don't think those girls who swarmed Friedbergs wanted to just chit chat. If they catch up to us, they'll be all over us like ants at a picnic."

"Great, huh, I've never had girls all over me like ants."

"Maybe ants is the wrong word. They're probably more like piranhas. They'd pick you clean in seconds."

"Hey! Since when are you such an expert on girls? Have you been holding out on me or something?"

"I'm not an expert. One or two are probably okay, but that crowd at Friedbergs was scary and Billy T said it was my job to keep you outta trouble. I think we should get out of here. It won't be long before those girls realize where we went. Besides, there are too many people here and some of them are staring at you like they're trying to remember where they've seen you before."

"Okay," Spazz said. "So let's get out of the mall. I'm thirsty. Let's go in here."

We were outside *The French Underground*. Another sign said *Paris Bistro*.

"I think it's a bar," I said.

"It's a restaurant too. Look there's a menu on the door. Come on, we'll grab a couple of Cokes."

We pushed open the door and went down a flight of stairs. A door at the bottom opened into a dimly lit bar and restaurant.

"We'll sit way at the back so we won't be noticed," Spazz announced.

"Okay," I said. "But I won't feel safe until we're back at the hotel."

We groped our way to a small table and sat down. It took a few minutes before my eyes adjusted to the darkness. Most of the light seemed to be coming from candles stuck in wine bottles on the tables. There were some people eating at the tables and a few more were sitting at a bar. I picked up a small menu as a young waitress wearing a very brief mini approached.

"Can I take your order?" The way she said order made me think she was French.

"Just a couple of Cokes," I said.

"Un sandwich, perhaps?"

"Sure. Why not?" Spazz said. "I'm a bit hungry, anyway. What have you got?"

"'Ere is the sandwich menu." She pointed to the menu in my hand. "We 'ave cold chicken, cold 'am and several o-ders."

"Yeah?" Spazz grinned. "What's your name? You really from France?"

"I am called Collette. But," she grinned, "I'm actually from Denver or, as we say in

France, Den-ver. I have …'ave to talk this way to work 'ere."

"No kidding?" Spazz said. "You sound like the real thing to me. Why don't you surprise us? Bring us a plate of your favourite sandwiches okay?"

"And two Cokes," I added. "Please."

"Hey. This is a neat place," Spazz said. "I bet Billy T eats here regular."

Collette returned a few minutes later with a plate of tiny sandwiches and two tall glasses of Coke and ice. "These are my favourite." She kept slipping in and out of her phony French accent. "But usually I would recommend a glass of *wyte* wine *wid dem* rather *dann* Coke."

"Yeah? Well we'll settle for Coke right now," Spazz said. "What is this pink stuff be-tween the bread?"

"Cream cheese and maraschino cherries. Uh, could I trouble you for your autograph?" Collette handed Spazz a slip of paper and a pen.

"Sure, why not? To Collette with love from Billy T." Spazz said the words as he wrote.

"Oh, thank you," Collette said. "Bon appetit."

As soon as Collette left, Spazz picked up a sandwich and took a bite. "You sure get to eat neat stuff when you're a rock star. This isn't half bad."

"Yeah?" I took a bite. "It's okay. But I think I'd settle for a Burger King burger instead. We could have bought about four each for the price of these sandwiches. I gotta go to the washroom. I'll be right back."

It took me a while to find the washroom in the gloom and when I returned, a woman in her thirties was sitting in my chair talking to Spazz.

"*Blondes at the Barricades* is expected to outsell even *Zero Tolerance*," she was saying. "How long did it take to get the album from first ideas to final cut? Oh, sorry," She'd noticed me. "I took your seat."

"That's okay." I pulled up another chair.

"Jessica Kendall," she extended her hand and I shook it. "Entertainment reporter for *The Chronicle*. And you are?"

"Kevin Ashworth. I'm one of Spazz's, uh Billy's roadies," I corrected, but she'd already lost all interest in me.

"Six months altogether," Spazz was saying. "From start to finish."

Jessica scribbled in a small notebook. "Just a couple more questions and then I'll leave you in peace. You've really been most understanding. You've no idea how difficult it is to get close to rock stars like yourself. On a personal note, could you give me any inkling who your latest is?"

"Well, it's like I said," Spazz said. "*Blondes at the Barricades*."

"No. I'm sorry. I didn't make myself clear. I meant your love life. If it's not too personal. Is it still on with Nirvana Nyx? She's becoming quite a star in her own right with a couple of hits on the charts right now. If you and she teamed up … and she is a blonde. Great publicity for your record. So? What shall I say? You haven't been seen with her in a while."

"Um, no," Spazz said. He caught my eye and saw me frowning at him. "Um. We've both been busy."

"Thanks. That's great. One last thing. I just happen to have a small camera in my purse. I know it's presumptuous of me but, just one picture?" She was already getting to her feet and fumbling with her camera. "Could you sit closer to Billy, er Eric?"

"It's Kevin," I said.

I took the chair Jessica had vacated. "I don't think this is a good idea," I whispered to Spazz, but Spazz had a big grin on his face and Jessica's camera flashed at the same instant.

"Thanks a million," Jessica said. "I'd no idea you were still in town and your agent refused all interviews at your last concert. You've really made my day. Bye."

"What was that all about?" I asked. "Billy T didn't say anything about giving interviews to the press. Let's get out of here before any more come. You've put in enough public appearances for one day. Let's get back to our hotel room, now."

"Okay, okay, I'm coming."

Spazz threw a number of bills on the table to pay for our lunch, stuffed the packet with the ties into his jacket pocket and followed me back out onto the mall. I took a quick look in both directions to make sure that the girls who had tried to mob us at Friedbergs weren't waiting for us.

I thought it best if we didn't follow the same route back and I hurried Spazz out the opposite side of the mall onto another street.

"That was dumb, giving an interview to a reporter. What do you know about Billy T's involvement with Nirvana Nyx?"

"Nothing. Except what I've read in *Rolling Stone.*"

"We've both been busy," I mimicked. "Good thing you didn't say anything about Vicky, the one you're supposed to be marrying. What else did you tell that woman before I got there?"

"Nothing much. Anyway she was convinced I was Billy T. How would it have looked if I'd told her I was plain old Bobby Spezzactena and I was just impersonating Billy T? You think she'd have believed me? And what would she have written then? I couldn't tell her about Billy T's wedding, now could I?"

"I guess not. But we'd better stay in our hotel room until Billy T comes back. That way, we'll stay outta trouble."

We had just reached the bottom of the steps

at the front door of The Ritz Plaza when we heard a squeal, "There he is!"

I glanced over my shoulder. The girls had caught up to us and were streaming across the street, weaving in and out of the traffic like it didn't exist.

"Come on," I grabbed Spazz's arm and propelled him up the steps and through the door even before the doorman had time to hold it open. We dashed across the lobby where Stanley was holding an elevator open for us. Before the elevator doors closed I saw several other Stanley-type guys hurry to join the doorman in case the girls, now clustering at the front door, attempted to enter.

We'd been back in our room about fifteen minutes and I was beginning to relax. I'd phoned my mom and told her I wouldn't be home for supper and that the job would last through Monday. She wasn't too happy to hear I'd be missing school, but I promised her I'd make it up – like do extra homework or something.

Spazz was studying the menu again, trying to decide what he'd order for supper although I couldn't see how he could possibly think of food. The girls had retreated across the street and were huddling on the corner again. There seemed to be more of them than before.

"We're okay," I said, "as long as we stay here. Those girls only get excited when they see you."

"It's too bad." Spazz sighed. "I've never had so many girls want me before. Maybe after this job's over I'll come downtown again dressed like this and let them have me. How could I arrange to meet them one at a time?"

"They might get angry if they found out who you really were and you might be a little worse for ..."

The door flew open with a crash. "There you are you no good son of a...." The door slammed shut, drowning out her last words. Even if the long blonde pony tail that reached her waist and her chain covered tight black leather dress weren't enough, the small green butterfly tattooed on her left cheek was a dead giveaway. It was Nirvana Nyx and she was mad.

"All right! Where is she? Have you got her stashed away in one of these bedrooms?"

She marched across the room and confronted Spazz. He'd risen nervously to his feet but Nirvana pushed him hard in the chest and he fell back into the armchair.

"I flew all the way from Atlanta when I realized what was going on. I was in the middle of a recording session too. Now! Do I have to search every room or are you gonna throw her out. I warn you. When I get my hands on her I'll pull every red hair from her pea-brained head.

"And as for you!" Nirvana picked up an expensive looking vase from a coffee table just as Spazz got to his feet again. She flung it at Spazz's head. Luckily he saw it coming and it smashed against the wall behind him. I wondered if we would have to pay for damages from the money Billy T gave us. Nirvana seemed to be searching for something else to throw at Spazz.

"She's not here and he's not Billy T," I blurted. I thought that a quick confession was best.

Nirvana was extremely strong for her size. I remembered reading somewhere she was into body building. She lifted a small end table off the floor.

"What? Who are you? I've never seen you before."

I was relieved to see her lower the table.

"I'm Kevin Ashworth and this is Bobby Spezzactena. We're just a couple of Eastridge High students. I know he looks like Billy T but he really isn't. Tell her Spazz."

Spazz said nothing. He seemed to be in a state of shock.

"Oh sure. You think I don't know this two-timing jerk." Nirvana seemed to have forgotten the coffee table but her eyes fell on a heavy glass ash tray on a nearby table.

"Let me explain," I said. "Billy T was here but he isn't here now. He wanted to go away for a few days and he needed someone to take his place, impersonate him. Spazz got the job because he looks like him."

"Let me see. I don't buy this for a minute."

Nirvana advanced on Spazz who had fallen into the chair again and seemed in a daze. I stood by nervously, hoping she wouldn't launch another attack. Her nails, done in gold to match her hair, looked awful long and dangerous.

She put her hands on the arms of Spazz's chair and peered into his eyes. "Well if you're not Billy, you're his double," she said quietly. "There's one way to know for certain."

I gasped and Spazz blinked with astonishment as she crawled onto his lap. She wrapped her arms around him and pressed herself against him. "Kiss me Billy," I heard her whisper. "Kiss me."

I gaped as Spazz and Nirvana locked in a passionate embrace although most of the passion seemed to be on Nirvana's side. Spazz was still in a state of shock.

Nirvana was kissing Spazz and he seemed to come out of his trance and start to respond. I wondered how long this test would last and what the next bit would be. It was embarrassing watching, but how many guys have seen their best friend neck with one of North America's bombshell female rock stars?

It was Nirvana who broke it off. She scrambled off Spazz's lap. "Okay, so you're not Billy T. You're a pretty good kisser whoever you are, but your technique is definitely not Billy T.'s. You've got sharper teeth or something. So where is the jerk?"

I had to answer. Spazz was sitting there with glazed eyes and a grin on his face, looking like someone who has just been told he won a million bucks.

"We don't know where he is," I said. "He didn't say where he was going."

"And I suppose Vicky was with him?"

I nodded.

"Oh well. I was mad when I got here, but what the heck. Maybe it's for the best. I hope she makes him happy the little ..." She laughed. "Sorry about the vase. Put it on Billy's bill. Tell him it's a wedding gift from me. Oh, I'm Nirvana, by the way."

"I know," I said.

"Another fan huh?"

"Yeah."

"You're kinda cute for a high school kid." She stroked my cheek and I blushed.

"How did you get past security?" I asked. "And past the guy outside?"

"I've been here lots of times with Billy. They know me. Billy didn't say to keep me out and I had my own key. Here. You can turn it in when you check out." She handed me the key. "Maybe you should put the safety chain on."

She laughed. "You don't want any more of Billy's girlfriends crashing in here. It might be dangerous for your friend."

"Thanks." I grinned. "That's a good idea."

My friend was still in the armchair looking spaced out. "Stay cool," Nirvana said as she left.

"Wow!" Spazz had returned to life. "Do you know who that was? That was Nirvana Nyx and I was kissing her. Can you believe it?"

"Yeah. But apparently not up to Billy T's standards." I grinned. "Luckily for you, or you might be dead."

"I thought I heard her say I was a pretty good kisser," Spazz said.

"Yeah? You sure? You looked out of it to me."

"Well. What did she say then?"

"Not enough tongue. And you should try taking the bubble gum out of your mouth first."

"You ..." It was Spazz's turn to look for something to throw, but before he could find anything, there was a knock at the door.

"I'll check it out," I said. "You didn't order anything did you?"

"Uh uh. Maybe it's Nirvana coming back for more. Maybe I got her really turned on."

"You wish."

Before I opened the door, I decided to peer through the spyhole. It was one of the maids. She was turned away from the door but I recognized the uniform and the little white hat thing on her head.

"Yes. What is it?" I asked.

"A manicure for Mr. Banko," the maid replied.

"It's a maid who says she's here for a manicure."

"Yeah?" Spazz grinned. "I've never given a maid a manicure before or anything else for that matter. Is she cute?"

"The manicure's for you, you klutz. Did you order one?"

"No. But what the heck, I've never had a manicure before either."

"Mr. Banko didn't order a manicure," I said through the door.

"It's complimentary. One of the services our hotel provides for its special guests."

"It's free," I told Spazz.

"Open the door," Spazz ordered. "Let her in! Every rock star needs a manicure. Can't have my nails snagging those old guitar strings, now can we? Open up. Don't leave the poor girl standing there. My nails are getting longer as we speak."

Playing Billy T was going to Spazz's head. He made me mad, ordering me around. "Open the door yourself! I may be your baby-sitter, but I'm not your servant." I stomped off to the bathroom.

SIX

I cooled off quick, but I took my time coming back. The maid was sitting on a foot stool beside Spazz working on his nails and he was grinning his fool head off. I didn't take much notice. I went towards the window intending to take another look at the girls across the street, but before I reached it, I heard the maid gasp.

What had dumb Spazz done now, I wondered. I turned and found a startled Lauren Malone looking at me.

It was my turn to gasp. "Lauren. What the...?"

She blushed but quickly recovered, frowning at me and shaking her head slightly which I took to mean, 'Don't give me away.' "Uh that's my sister's name," she said. "I'm Susan."

"Oh? You know Susan's sister, do you Kevin?" Spazz asked in a phony voice. Then he couldn't contain himself any longer. He burst out laughing.

Lauren got to her feet, startled. "I'm sorry Mr. Banko … I … Wait a minute. You're… Are you? Kevin, what's going on? You're here and… Oh no! You and Spazz skipped school today and … Is that you, Spazz? You jerk, I've never been so humiliated. You! … You! …You just sat there all this time letting me do your nails, pretending to be Billy T Banko. You creep!"

Spazz was doubled up with laughter. "Do you do massages too?" he roared.

It was lucky that Nirvana Nyx had already smashed the only vase within reach because Lauren looked like she was ready to break something over Spazz's head if there'd been anything handy.

"How could you do this to me?" She turned to me. "Is this your idea of a joke, Kevin Ashworth? Because I think it stinks. How could you be so mean?"

Lauren covered her face with her hands and I thought she was about to burst out crying. I punched Spazz on the arm to shut him up and his laughter slowed to a splutter and stopped altogether when he looked at Lauren.

"It's not a joke, Lauren," I said quietly. "Me and Spazz got this job. We didn't know you were going to walk in here dressed as a maid. It wasn't planned."

Spazz heard the concern in my voice. "Kevin's right, Lauren. Here, would you like something to drink?" Spazz got to his feet. "We've got a whole bar, anything you want. A brandy, maybe?"

"Oh Spazz, you dummy, I'm upset. But I'm not going to faint." Lauren had removed her hands from her face. She wasn't crying but I saw a tear glisten in her eye. She forced a smile. "A diet Pepsi would be fine. No. Wait. I'd better get out of here. This is my sister's uniform. She works here part-time. It's her weekend off and she mentioned that Billy T Banko was staying here. I've made a real fool of myself, I'd better go." She got to her feet.

"It's okay," I said. "Your sister was right. Billy was here. This is his suite. But he went away secretly for the weekend. Billy wanted someone to pretend he was still here and Spazz looked enough like him to get the job. Spazz met him at the concert. I'm sorry I screwed up getting the tickets. I didn't think you were such a big Black Vulture fan until I took you to that movie. Sorry."

"It's okay. But I'd better go. I don't want my sister to lose her job. This whole idea was dumb. I'd better get home and get this uniform back before she discovers I borrowed it."

"Don't go yet. Have that drink. Nobody

knows you're here anyway, except maybe the guy outside the door. Does anyone else?"

"Actually, I came up the back stairs. There was no one outside the door when I knocked. He must have gone to the bathroom or taken a coffee break or something."

"I'm sorry, Lauren," Spazz said. "No hard feelings. I just couldn't resist when you walked in that door. I wanted to see if you'd recognize me. It was tough though, trying not to laugh. Sorry, but it was funny. I promise, not a word of this shall pass my lips. No one at Eastridge High will ever know, except me and Kevin," Spazz went to the bar. "Come on. The drink's on Billy T anyway. But I can't find any diet Pepsi here. Want me to call room service?"

"No. Don't you dare! All right. What have you got? I'll have one drink and then I'll go. But I'll hold you to your promise Spazz. You too, Kevin. I'd die if anyone at Eastridge found out about this."

"Scout's honour," Spazz said. "But what about when I'm old? What a story to tell my grandchildren. The weekend I spent in the Royal Suite of the best hotel in town with the cutest maid in the place."

"Spaaaazz," Lauren said warningly. "Okay. I'll stay for one drink and you guys can fill me in on what you're doing here and then give me a quick tour of the place. Okay, Spazz let's see what you've got."

"We've got lots of stuff. Here's something called Parfait Amour, how about a shot of that?" Spazz held up a small bottle of clear purple liquid. "I think it's what they call a liqueur. It's French. Or there's 7-Up, wine, ginger ale, and much more. Come see for yourself."

"I wouldn't mind trying a taste of that purple stuff. But just a teeny bit."

"Anything you say, mademoiselle." Spazz put on his best imitation of a French accent as he filled a tiny, narrow glass with the purple liquid and handed it to Lauren. "A French drink for a French maid."

"Oh, knock it off, Spazz." Lauren took a small sip. "Hmm, it's kinda sweet. Tastes kinda like violets. Not bad."

We were all trying a taste of Parfait Amour when the door flew open again with a loud bang. I jumped. I turned quickly to look and I gasped. This time, I knew it was real trouble. The two guys who burst in were carrying guns and wore ski masks over their faces.

Lauren was taking a sip of her drink and she was so startled she took a big gulp and started choking.

The bigger of the two guys kicked the door closed behind him and waved us to sit down by motioning with his gun.

"What is this?" Spazz gasped.

"Shut up and sit," the big guy snapped.

Spazz went to the armchair. Lauren was

still spluttering and coughing, trying to catch her breath. I helped her to a couch.

"Are you okay?"

She nodded and tried to speak but started coughing again. "Is this another part — cough — cough — part of your crazy job, Kevin? — cough — cough — because if it is some kind of joke, I don't — cough — cough — want any part of it."

I cursed myself for not putting the safety chain on the door like Nirvana Nyx had suggested. "I've no idea who these guys are, Lauren, honest —"

"I said shut up," the big guy snapped again. "And stop coughing for crying out loud, you're making me nervous."

The other one seemed even more nervous. He kept pointing his gun at me, then Lauren, then Spazz and back at me again.

Lauren gave a few more splutters, then seemed to catch her breath. "Who do you think you are, barging in like this — and stop pointing those guns. They might go off, you jerks."

"Hey," the big guy growled. "Don't give us no lip and you won't get hurt." He walked over to Lauren and grabbed her chin in his left hand and laid the snub-nosed barrel of the small black pistol on her cheek. "What are you doin' here anyway? Having a little drinky-winky with the boys? The hotel manager wouldn't like that, now would he?"

"Leave her alone," I said.

"Yeah? You gonna make me?" The pistol moved from Lauren's face to just under my nose. I shut up. I realized these guys were serious. The gun was cold against my skin, sending shivers up my spine and I could hear my heart pounding in my ears.

"Come on Melvin, Glory said we shouldn't take long," the smaller one said. "You." He pointed at Spazz. "You're Billy T Banko, right?"

"Uh no, actually," Spazz said.

"Of course he is," said the one we now knew as Melvin. "Who else would he be? I don't know who this other guy is, but we only want Billy-boy, here."

"I just want to be sure, that's all," the smaller guy went on. "We don't want no screw ups. Remember Glory said to check that picture on that magazine article."

Melvin fumbled in the side pocket of the brown tweed jacket he was wearing and pulled out a folded magazine page. He flipped it open. "Relax, Nosh. It's him all right. See for yourself. The spitting image." He passed the page over to the one he called Nosh.

Nosh studied it and grunted in agreement.

"What do you guys want?" I asked.

"Just your friend here. He's going for a little ride with us. He won't get hurt if he co-operates. We're just gonna hold him for a little while until his agent comes up with a little cash. Then we'll let him go."

"You mean this is a kidnapping?" Lauren gasped.

"You got it," Melvin said. "You're a smart maid."

"I'm not a maid," Lauren said, angrily. She nodded at Spazz. "And he's not Billy T Banko."

"She's right," I added. "All three of us are just high school kids. We go to the same school."

Melvin started laughing. "That's rich. 'We're just three high school kids. We go to the same school.'" He mimicked my voice. "That's really rich, hey Nosh? Ain't that rich? You know Nosh, if we ever make it to the big time, we can stay in a place like this." He turned back to us, waved his gun and growled. "How dumb do you think we are? I suppose you'll tell us next that this is just a twenty-buck-a-night hotel room and that The Ritz Plaza always rents out rooms like this for weekends to high school kids out of the goodness of its heart. Not to mention throwing in a maid to fool around with."

"I'm not a maid and I wasn't fooling around, you pig." Lauren blushed and she sounded really mad.

"Just another little high school girl, huh?" Melvin scoffed.

"Melvin. What are we gonna do with the girl and this other guy?" Nosh asked.

"We'll take them down the back stairs to the parking lot and when we get to the car, we'll let this little chicky and her friend go. We weren't counting on having to take any prisoners, but it will only be temporary. Speaking of prisoners, you'd better check out the other rooms, Nosh."

Nosh came back a minute later, "No one there, Melvin."

"I'm really not Billy T Banko," Spazz said. "You're making a big mistake."

"Take off the wig, Spazz," I said. "Show them."

"Don't make any fast moves now," Melvin warned and levelled the pistol at Spazz.

Spazz reached up and slowly removed his wig. "See,"

"So?" Melvin said. "So Billy T Banko wears a wig. What of it?"

"My name is Bobby Spezzactena, not Billy T Banko. I just happen to look like him —"

"We're wasting time. Now all three of you are goin' to get up slowly and walk to the door. Nosh and me will be right behind you."

"He doesn't look like Billy T Banko anymore, Melvin." Nosh was studying the picture again. "You sure it's him? We don't want no mistakes. Glory will be mad."

"What a dummy. Of course he's Billy T Banko. Lots of these rock stars wear wigs. Here give me that article. I'll prove it to you that he's the genuine goods."

"What about your wallet, Spazz? Show him some I.D.," I urged.

"I didn't bring any I.D.," Spazz said. "I didn't think I'd need it."

"Well then, show him the card. The one Billy gave you."

"Billy has it. I left it in my jacket."

I groaned.

Nosh had handed Melvin the magazine page and Melvin was studying it.

"Here," he said. He pointed to the article. "This will prove it. It says here that, 'The leader of Black Vulture, Billy T Banko, sports a small black vulture tattooed on his right arm.' Okay you. Roll up your sleeve."

Lauren and I looked at each other and breathed a sigh of relief.

"The other sleeve, dummy," Melvin growled.

We looked at Spazz who shrugged and slowly rolled up his right sleeve. I nearly died and I heard Lauren gasp. There, tattooed on Spazz's arm, was a black vulture's head.

SEVEN

Spazz shrugged apologetically as Lauren and I stared at the tattoo.

"Okay, Nosh," Melvin said. "There's the proof. You satisfied? This guy is definitely Billy T Banko."

I finally got over the shock enough to ask, "When did you get that tattoo, Spazz? And why? They're never gonna believe us now."

"Sorry guys. I got it just after Billy T hired me. I figured if I was going to play him, I should look as authentic as possible."

Lauren groaned. "You klutz Spazz. You've really done it now. I thought you had to be over eighteen to get a tattoo anyway."

"I lied. I'm sorry. The guy in the tattoo shop didn't seem to care anyway. Sorry. Any other ideas?"

"Maybe you should let this guy kiss you, Like Nirvana Nyx did," I said scornfully.

"Okay. Enough talk," Melvin said. "Nosh, take a quick look outside and see if the coast is clear. Now you three, get up and walk real slow."

"It's all clear, Melvin," Nosh whispered from the door. I wondered what had happened to the guy who had been sitting outside. Lauren had said he wasn't there when she'd arrived, but if he'd just gone for coffee he was taking an awful long time.

Nosh held the door open as Melvin herded us out into the hall.

"Walk slow. Down the hall to the stairs," Melvin pointed with his gun. Nosh closed the door to the room behind him, then hurried ahead of us.

I led the rest of the group, followed by Lauren, then Spazz, with Melvin bringing up the rear with his gun in Spazz's back.

Nosh pulled open the door to the stairs and I heard him draw in his breath. There was some commotion down below and I got a quick look over his shoulder. The guy who had been guarding our room, Stanley and another guy dressed like him were trying to hold back a mob of squealing and screaming girls. The staircase seemed to be packed with them. They began chanting, "We want Billy! We want Billy!"

"What's goin' on?" Melvin muttered. He

pushed his way forward to take a look and, as he did so, Lauren tried to push past him, yelling, "Help," down the stairwell. I don't think anyone would have heard her, the noise from the girls was so loud, but Melvin slapped a hand over Lauren's mouth and pushed her roughly back before slamming the door.

He waved the gun at us. "Everyone back to the room."

We were hustled down the hall again and I heard Nosh ask in a worried voice, "What do we do now, Melvin?"

"Shut up Nosh. I've got to think. Open the door," Melvin snarled. "Come on. Hurry up. Who's got the key?"

We all looked at one another and I saw Nosh shrug.

"Come on, come on." Melvin said. "Don't play games with me. Open the door. Now which one of you has the key?"

"I left it in the room," Spazz said.

"Search them, Nosh," Melvin said.

The noise from the stairs grew louder.

"Oh forget it. Stand back. Nosh. You keep them covered."

Nosh waved his pistol at us as Melvin aimed his boot at the door and gave it a hard kick. I wondered if we'd have to pay for the damage to the door as well as the vase Nirvana broke. It took Melvin three tries before the door flew open and we were hustled inside again.

"Everyone sit," Melvin yelled. "I've got to think. Not you, Nosh, you dummy. You keep them covered."

We sat in the same places we'd occupied before, as Melvin paced up and down muttering to himself.

He stopped pacing and said aloud, "We've only got two choices. The stairs are out. That leaves the elevator and we'd have to go out through the lobby, or we can hole up here and wait until they clear that mob on the stairs. Who are those girls anyway? You know anything about this?" He looked at Spazz.

"They're Black Vulture fans," Spazz said. "They think Billy T is here."

"They're right. Everyone and their dog wants to get in on this act. I'll have to talk to Glory. She'll know what to do." He pulled a Walkie Talkie out of his jacket pocket. "Glory. Glory, come in Glory."

There was a squawk from the Walkie Talkie, then a faint tinny voice said something. Melvin held it up to his ear then started talking rapidly, explaining to whoever Glory was that the back stairs were blocked. The tinny voice seemed to get higher and I saw Melvin wince. Then he said, "Okay. We'll do like you say. We'll give it a try."

He switched off the Walkie Talkie and put it in his pocket.

"Glory says we've got to go out through the

lobby. As well as that mob of girls on the stairs, there's another crowd of them beginning to collect on the street. Glory says if we don't get out of here now, it'll be too late. She says the hotel has probably already called the cops to help control the girls and the whole place will be crawling with them soon. If we stay here, we'll be trapped. The cops will come up here to check and see if Billy T is okay. So, Nosh, here's the plan. We all go down in the elevator and we stick real close together. We act like we're getting Billy T outta the hotel, like we're his bodyguards."

"Waving guns and wearing ski-masks!" Lauren laughed.

"Shaddup," Melvin said. "We keep our guns in our pockets, but they'll be pointed at you all the time. Any fast moves and you're dead. Glory says we'll have to take off our ski masks. It can't be helped. We'll be long gone with Billy-boy before they realize what is happening. Glory is gonna meet us out on the street with the car. Okay, you two guys get your jackets on. We want this to look as natural as possible. It's cool outside and it wouldn't look right walking out in only shirts and pants. And you," he pointed at Spazz. "You may as well put your wig back on. If they think we are taking you to safety away from those screaming girls, so much the better."

Spazz and I picked up our jackets from the

back of the couch where we'd left them earlier and slipped them on.

Spazz jammed the wig on his head. Melvin came over and turned it around. Spazz had put it on backwards, deliberately.

"Leave Lauren here," I said. "You don't need her."

"She's coming to the front door with us. It will look all the more natural with a hotel maid walking across the lobby. Okay, take off your mask, Nosh."

"Okay Melvin."

Nosh pulled his ski-mask off as Melvin did the same. Nosh was a dark-haired guy with dark bulging eyes and big ears. He grinned at us sheepishly. Melvin had a brush cut, a big nose and a missing front tooth. He looked like a bouncer from a nightclub, but I guessed he could pass for a bodyguard. He looked big and mean enough.

"Put your ski-mask in your pocket, Nosh. We don't want to leave no evidence behind, and put your gun in there too. Okay, now you, the maid, you lead the way. Then Nosh and then you two guys. No. Bunch up. Real close. That's it. Hang onto each other. Nosh. You hang onto the maid. Okay. Let's try walking out of here."

We must have looked like a giant crab or a football huddle as we shambled forward. We were bunched up so close together it was hard to walk properly. But it might work, I thought dismally. Anyone seeing us crossing the lobby all bunched up might think it was a clutch of security types surrounding someone important and being led by one of the hotel maids.

As we walked to the elevators, it sounded like the ruckus in the stairwell was still going on. I hoped that the elevator would take ages to come or when it did it would be full of cops. Of course, it arrived almost immediately and was empty. We shuffled inside, still in a bunch, and then Melvin rearranged us again because otherwise we would have had to stumble out backwards into the lobby.

We watched the numbers of the floors as they lit up. I hoped we would stop at lots of floors and the elevator would get packed with people, giving one of us a chance to whisper, "We're being kidnapped." Maybe we could even yell out.

Would Melvin fire off shots in the elevator to silence us? If he did, would security grab him and Nosh when they stepped into the lobby? I didn't get a chance to find out. The elevator didn't stop at any of the other floors.

As the L for lobby lit up, Melvin said, "Easy now. Stick real close together. Don't say nothin' to nobody. Just walk straight ahead to the front door and nobody will get hurt."

The doors slid open with a faint hiss.

"Easy now," Melvin growled. "Remember

no tricks."

The whole group moved into the lobby as one. We started shambling across the plush carpet towards the front doors. I scanned the lobby. Everything looked normal. Nobody took any notice of us. Where were Stanley's security guys in their blue Arabian Nights outfits? I couldn't see any. Were they all battling the girls on the stairs? And where was that Maitre D' guy? He'd stopped Spazz and me on the way into the hotel. Why couldn't he do his job now and stop us on the way out?

I couldn't believe it. We were being completely ignored. People were checking in and out at the front desk. Porters were loading luggage onto trolleys. Hotel patrons crossed the lobby like we were invisible. Everyone seemed intent on their own thoughts. Nobody noticed a major kidnapping was in progress. Even the dumb orchestra went on playing and people at the dining tables went on sipping their wine and feeding their faces.

We were just about past the last of the dining tables when a figure leaped up in front of us.

"Lauren! What is this? You work here? I'm sorry. It's such a shock. I guess you need the extra money or something, but a maid?"

It was Debbie Dobrazynski. Our little group had come to a dead stop.

"I'm celebrating my sixteenth birthday,"

Debbie went on. "My father invited me and a few of my friends out for dinner. Why are you making such weird faces Lauren? Kevin!" She'd spotted me. "What are you doing here? Is this some kind of frosh initiation or something like that? It can't be. We went through that last year. It's a fancy dress deal, right?"

"Who is this crazy dame?" I heard Melvin mutter. "Everyone move."

No one did. Nosh was standing there, looking a bit bewildered, a silly grin on his face and Debbie was going on again.

"Who else is here?" She peered into the group and caught sight of Spazz. "Who is that? You know he looks just like, what's his name? You know?" She looked back at Lauren for help. "Spazz? Really? You're kidding. I thought he was … Oh what a laugh."

I figured Lauren must have told her but behind us Melvin was getting real impatient. "I said move," he snarled. He pushed me and Spazz and the whole group surged forward. Nosh and Lauren stumbled into Debbie.

"How rude," she snapped crossly as she suddenly found herself in the centre of the group being carried towards the door.

"Hey, what's going on? Who's pushing?" Debbie asked. Then she gave a little squeal as Melvin grabbed her arm and I figured he must have also poked her with his pistol. She shut up, went pale and I felt her stagger against me.

I thought she was going to faint but she stayed on her feet and kept moving. She hadn't much choice. She was jammed in the middle of the group.

Suddenly we were at the door and I couldn't believe my eyes. The doorman was holding it open for us. As soon as we got outside, he ran down the steps ahead of us helping to make a path through a cluster of screaming girls. Then I saw where the other Arabian Nights guys were. They were doing their best to hold back the girls and prevent them from coming up the steps.

The girls spotted Spazz and surged forward screaming, "There he is! Oh Billy! I love you," and several other screams I couldn't make out. It was bedlam.

The doorman shouldered his way through another pack of girls and we got to the sidewalk. A limo was pulling up to the curb. The doorman already had his hand on the handle of one of the doors to open it for us, when a beaten up green four-door Ford screeched to a stop in front of it.

The driver leaned across and pushed open the front door on the passenger side. Here's where we make a break for it I thought, or, at least Lauren gets free. But at that moment Debbie decided to faint. Before I knew what was happening, Melvin had pushed Lauren and Nosh onto the front seat and slammed the door. The doorman, realizing we weren't going to take the limo, and apparently thinking that the battered heap was a decoy car to fool any fans who were on the street, flung open the back door and helped bundle us in. I was jammed against the far door and Spazz landed on top of me. Before I could get my breath back, Melvin was in the car. I knew from the bulge in his pocket that the gun was pointed at me and Spazz but Melvin seemed to be struggling to free himself from Debbie. Although she'd fainted, she was somehow clinging to Melvin. The top half of her was in the car on his lap and the rest of her was sprawled on the sidewalk.

Melvin tried to get Debbie off him but the dumb doorman, thinking he was being helpful, boosted the rest of her into the car on top of us. The door slammed and the driver, a woman with cropped blonde hair, floored the accelerator. As we sped away, I could hear the sound of police sirens approaching the hotel. Stanley and his crew must have called for reinforcements. Where were the cops when we needed them? I wondered. Then I saw. A cop stood in the middle of the street at the next intersection and the traffic light was red for us.

We're saved, I thought. Then I couldn't believe it.

The cop raised his hand, stopped the oncoming traffic and waved us through the intersection.

EIGHT

"Couldn't you two do anything right? Do I have to do everything myself?"

Glory spun the steering wheel and the car zipped around a slow-moving delivery van. I noticed when she glanced in the rear view mirror that she had startlingly blue eyes and she looked to be in her mid-twenties. "I ask you to pick up one guy and you bring half the staff of The Ritz Plaza."

"We only brought one maid," Melvin protested. "We had to. We used her to get through the lobby."

"I'm — not — a — maid," Lauren muttered through clenched teeth.

"Well, what about the other two?" Glory continued. "How many Billy T Bankos do you think there are? What did you do? Bring a whole collection so I could choose one? And what's wrong with that one lying down on top of you in the back?" Glory swore as she swerved to avoid a cyclist who had just pulled out from the curb. "I told you not to use violence."

"She fainted," Melvin said.

"It's her birthday, Glory," Nosh added.

"We can dump the maid and the other two at the next corner," Melvin said.

"I'm not a maid," Lauren yelled. "And no one in this car is Billy T Banko."

"What's this dame yelling about?" Glory snapped. "That is the right guy back there, isn't it? The black-haired guy? If you and Nosh screwed up again, Melvin I'll ..."

"It's the right guy," Melvin answered, "Look, pull over at the next corner and let's get rid of these others."

"Are you crazy? There are cops all over the place. Look there's another one waving us through this intersection. I don't know what's going on, but this is a gas. The cops are actually helping us."

Glory waved her thanks at the cop as she passed. "The hotel must have told the cops that Billy T left in this car. They don't know we've grabbed him. They must think we're just getting him away from those crazy girls. The cops probably radioed ahead to let us through. Here's another one. Everybody wave."

Glory, Nosh, Lauren and I waved and the cop waved back. The trouble was that the cop didn't know the difference between waves for help, Lauren's and mine, and waves of thanks, Glory's and Nosh's. Spazz didn't wave. I think he was still a bit dazed or his arms were trapped under Debbie's limp body. Melvin didn't wave either. He still had one hand in his pocket holding the gun, and he was using the other hand to cover Debbie's face so the cop wouldn't notice her if he looked in the car as we sped by.

"We're gonna have to hang onto everyone," Glory said. "If we let any of them out, they'll blow the whistle on us right away. All they have to do is tell the nearest cop what's happened and they'll be after us. The cops obviously know what this car looks like."

"You're making a big mistake," I said.

"Shut up," Melvin said. "Let's not start that again."

"He's right, Glory," Lauren said. "The guy in the back is Bobby Spezzactena, not Billy T Banko. He's just a high school kid. We all are. Melvin and Nosh did screw up. Really."

"Nice try, but give me a break," Glory said. "The cops don't stop traffic for a bunch of high school kids in a beat up old Ford."

Debbie was beginning to stir and she obviously disliked having Melvin's hand on her face. Melvin suddenly let out a yelp. It was lucky we were now out of the downtown area, because Melvin's yelp startled Glory and the car swerved violently.

"What's goin' on back there?" she yelled as she got the car under control again. "Do you want to get us all killed?"

"This little so-and-so bit me." Melvin was sucking on his hand.

"Get all of them down on the floor. I can't concentrate on my driving. They don't need to see where we're going anyway. We'll blindfold them as soon as it's safe to pull over, but we'll need some more blindfolds. I wasn't counting on four of them. Now get them down."

Melvin pushed Debbie off him onto the floor at our feet and she hollered, "What's going on?" He then pulled the gun out of his pocket and motioned Spazz and me to get down. We scrunched down behind the front seat and helped Debbie sit up. It was a tight squeeze with the three of us and Melvin's big legs and feet taking up so much room. In the front, I heard Lauren protest and Glory say, "Sit on her if you have to."

Debbie was now almost fully awake. "What's going on you guys? My father's going to be really mad at me for skipping out on my party. My friends are going to think me awfully rude. Where's Lauren? I was going to ask her to join my sorority Phi Kappa Delta, but not after this," Debbie babbled on, sounding delirious.

Probably suffering from shock, I thought. "Anyway, I don't think the other girls would vote her in, once they realized she's a hotel maid. We do have certain standards."

"Thanks a lot, Debbie." It was Lauren. Her voice seemed to come from under the seat so I guessed she was on the floor too. "Despite the fact that I'm not a maid, even if you begged me to join, I wouldn't join your stinking sorority. Not now, anyway."

"Lauren is that you?" Debbie asked. She seemed to have fully recovered now. "Why are we sitting on the floor of this grungy car? I'm getting my new dress all dirty." She struggled to get up but Melvin stepped on her. It was then she noticed the gun being pointed at her. She gave a gasp and I thought she might faint again. "Is this for real, Spazz? That is you Spazz, isn't it?"

Spazz nodded, "It's for real. They made a mistake. They think I'm Billy T Banko, you know, Black Vulture."

"So that's who you look like, I couldn't remember. But haven't you told them?"

Spazz nodded.

"Well tell them again. Hey, you creep. I know this guy. He's Bobby Spezzactena. He goes to my school. He always dresses weird. And this other kid is Kevin Ashworth. And I guess Lauren Malone is in the front seat. I'm sorry Lauren about what I said. I'm not sure what I was talking about."

"Forget it," I heard Lauren mutter. "Save your breath."

"Okay," Debbie went on talking to Melvin. "So now you know. Would you mind taking your grimy foot off me and let us out of this car. You hear me?" Debbie raised her voice when she got no response. "Let us out!"

Melvin didn't like being yelled at by Debbie. He pressed down harder with his foot.

"Oh, you're hurting me. Get off me."

"You be quiet then," Melvin snarled. But he eased his foot off her leg.

"It's no use, Debbie," I said. "We've tried to persuade them that Spazz is just Spazz but they won't listen. They're sure he's Billy T Banko."

"How dumb can they be? Of course he's Spazz. Everyone knows he's Spazz," Debbie hollered.

"Keep it down back there," Glory yelled. "I'm going to pull over. If they don't shut up, we'll have to gag them. That one in the back in particular is getting on my nerves. Tell her Melvin, if she doesn't shut up, she'll have to ride in the trunk."

Debbie gasped but said no more. I felt the car slow down, then ease to a stop.

"Okay," Glory said. "All of you in the back, stay where you are. You keep them in there, Melvin. Now Nosh, give me your gun. Okay. Now in the glove compartment you'll find a couple of strips of cloth. Okay, blindfold the maid first."

"I know I look like a maid, but I'm not a maid. I'm just Lauren Malone, ordinary high school kid." Lauren sounded exasperated.

"Yeah. And I'm Little Red Riding Hood," Glory scoffed. "Shut up, will ya. Tie it tight, Nosh. That's it. Here's another strip of cloth, Melvin. Here, Nosh. Take your gun back. Melvin give me yours. I'll keep them covered. We need to find a couple more strips of cloth for the other two. What's that gabby one wearing? She got a slip on?" Glory got out of the car and came around to the back door on the other side and opened it.

"You're not taking my slip," Debbie protested.

"Let her out of the car, Melvin. She won't be able to take her slip off sitting on the floor." Glory said.

Debbie continued to protest as Melvin prodded her out of the car and then followed. "But it's brand new." Debbie was outside the car but I couldn't see anything. There was a sound of tearing cloth. "You witch," I heard Debbie say.

"You shut your mouth," Glory ordered. "Or you're gonna have the rest of this slip stuffed in your mouth."

A blindfolded Debbie was bundled into the car beside us and then Melvin reached in and put blindfolds on Spazz and me. It was scary, not to be able to see and Melvin had tied the blindfold real tight. It pinched the hair on the back of my head.

"Okay," Glory said. "We'd better get going. Make sure they stay down. And listen up, you four. If any of you try to pull off your blindfolds, Melvin or Nosh will club you over the head with their pistols."

Glory started the car again and I swayed against Debbie as it moved off. It felt weird, moving without being able to see where we were going and only hearing the rumble of the engine.

"Melvin," Glory said. "When we unload our cargo and get them safely locked up, you're gonna have to take this car and dump it. Too many cops know it, and when they wake up to what's happened, they'll come looking for it."

We drove in silence for what seemed like about half an hour, each of us wrapped up in our own thoughts. It was strange. All sorts of plans for escape should have been racing through my head but all I could think of was Debbie. I could smell her perfume. Here I was, practically lying beside the girl of my dreams, blindfolded with a piece of her perfumed slip. It's funny the fantasies that go through your head when you're kidnapped, but then I'd never been kidnapped before.

The car lurched to a stop. I felt cool air on

my face as the doors were opened. Someone grabbed my arm and pulled. I found I had pins and needles in one foot and when I tried to walk it felt like I had a large spring attached to the sole of that foot. It was difficult to walk, what with being blindfolded, too. I knew it must be Melvin who had a hold of my arm. I'd got used to the smell of his sweat in the car. There were other footsteps nearby and the scrunch of gravel so I guessed the others were being led also.

A door creaked and then slammed behind me. Melvin still had a hold of my arm. The surface beneath my feet felt different, smoother, and there was a musty smell in the air that wasn't Melvin.

I heard a strange sliding sound, then a crash and I was pushed forward. The sliding sound came again and another crash, then suddenly I felt myself shoot upward. I realized I was in an elevator, I could also hear the whine of the motor. We stopped with a jerk. I'd no idea how many floors we'd risen. There was the sliding crashing sound again, which I now guessed must be the door of the elevator. I was pushed forward, stumbling and falling against someone else.

I put my hands out to stop myself and found I was on what felt like a hard wooden floor. The elevator door crashed shut and again there was the whine of the motor. I waited a moment. I thought I could hear breathing.

"Anyone here?" I asked.

"Me." It was Lauren's voice.

"Me too," Spazz and Debbie said together.

"I think they've gone," Lauren said. Then more loudly she said, "I'm taking off my blindfold, is that okay?"

No one answered. I reached up and pulled off my blindfold. Lauren, Spazz and Debbie had done the same.

We were lying on the rough, wooden, dusty floor of a huge empty room. The floor was stained with oil and paint spills. There was a row of small barred windows, high up along one wall and I could see it was nearly dark outside. Close to where we lay was an open elevator shaft. I crawled towards the opening and looked down. I could see the elevator way below. It looked at least five storeys down.

"Where are we?" Lauren asked.

"I think it's an old warehouse," I said.

"There's a door over here but it's locked," Spazz said.

I joined him and we threw ourselves against it, but it was hopeless.

"I think it's nailed shut or boarded up on the other side," I said.

Outside, there was the sound of a car driving away. Lauren and Spazz ran to the windows, Spazz boosted Lauren up in an effort to see out, but the windows were too high.

"This is some sixteenth birthday," Debbie sighed.

"Many happy returns," Lauren said scornfully.

NINE

It grew dark. There were a couple of yellowed plastic lamp shades hanging from the ceiling, but no bulbs. Before it got totally dark all four of us lay on our stomachs at the edge of the elevator shaft and peered down. It was hard to see much. A faint glimmer of light entered the shaft at three other locations. Above us there was just the roof of the shaft.

"I think we're on the fifth floor of the building," I said. "This room is the entire fifth floor. Those bits of light are coming in from the fourth, third and second floors. The elevator must be on the main floor and it's blocking the light there. You can just see the top of it."

"It's scary-looking," Debbie said. "What if we'd fallen down there with our blindfolds on? I hope nobody here sleepwalks."

"There's no way we could climb down," I said. "How come there aren't any cables anyway? What makes this thing go up and down?"

"It probably works on hydraulics," Spazz said. "It's kinda the same as a car hoist in a service station. It gets pushed up from underneath. There's one like it in my aunt's apartment in New York. How far do you figure it is down to the next floor?"

"At least twenty feet," I said. "We'll take a better look when it's light. We'd better stay well back. We don't want any accidents."

We moved back and sat under the windows with our backs against the wall.

We talked. Debbie wanted to know all the details of what had happened. She said if she had the same information as the rest of us, maybe we could put our heads together to come up with a plan to get us out of there.

I did most of the talking with Lauren adding a bit here and there, Spazz said nothing. I think he was too embarrassed about everything that had happened. I even mentioned Nirvana Nyx, but I didn't say how she found out Spazz wasn't Billy T.

When we'd finished, Spazz said, "Sorry guys, I never intended any of this to happen. I feel really dumb, especially getting that tattoo. We would have been off the hook if it wasn't for that."

"You couldn't know you were gonna get

kidnapped," Lauren said. "I sure didn't when I borrowed my sister's maid uniform. I guess she wouldn't be allowed in your sorority either, huh, Debbie? She's really a maid. You see, she has this thing about putting herself through college, so she works part time at The Ritz. Though maybe you could hire her, Debbie," Lauren went on sarcastically, "next time you need a maid to serve the hors d'oeuvres at your sorority's get-together."

"Look, I don't know exactly what I said in the car. There is no sorority. I don't know what I was babbling on about. I was confused and upset. I might join a sorority when I get to university, but right now, I don't know of one. I apologize, Lauren, for whatever I said. Look, let's not fight. We've all got to work together to get out of this jam — okay?"

"Okay," Lauren said. "Debbie's right. We can't just sit here. We've gotta make some plans. Listen. What's that?"

There was the sound of a car pulling up outside. "Someone's coming," Lauren said. "They probably got rid of the Ford and brought back a different vehicle. It sounds noisier."

We sat in silence, listening. A few minutes later there was the sound of the elevator rising. When it arrived, Glory and Nosh were in it. Nosh pushed back the meshed door as Glory shone a flashlight on us. There was a strong smell of pizza and I suddenly realized how hungry I was.

"Stay where you are. I've got a gun. We've brought you some blankets and food. Here." Glory tossed a small pile of blankets at us. "Okay, Nosh. Put the pizza on the floor."

Nosh stepped into the room and put a couple of cardboard boxes and a paper bag on the floor and then stepped back into the elevator.

"So. It's not The Ritz Plaza." Glory laughed. "But you're not paying either. You don't even have to tip." She was about to close the elevator door.

"Wait," Debbie said. "I have to go to the bathroom."

"All right," Glory said. "Get in. I guess we'd better get this over with. Everyone can go to the bathroom once. Then you'll have to wait 'till morning. I'll be back for you one at a time."

Debbie stepped into the elevator. Glory closed the door, pulled a lever and the elevator disappeared.

"Hey, listen you guys," I said. "When you go to the bathroom, keep your eyes open. Look at everything and try to remember what you see. We'll compare notes. Maybe we can find a way out of here."

Glory and Nosh returned with Debbie and Lauren left. We decided to wait until everyone was back before attacking the pizza. The paper bag contained four cans of cold pop and one cupcake with white icing and sprinkles.

Spazz left next and then it was my turn. The elevator moved slower than I'd thought when I rode in it blindfolded. I was right about the number of floors. On the ground floor, Melvin was sitting at a table listening to a small portable radio. The room was sparsely furnished. A table, two chairs and an empty crate was all it contained. Melvin got up and he and Nosh led me down a narrow hallway to a toilet. Glory handed me a metal pail to take back to the room. "Just in case anyone gets desperate during the night. We hadn't planned on four of you."

Five minutes later I was back in the room with the others. I set the pail down in one corner. "A present from Glory," I said. "In case anyone can't hold out 'till morning."

"Oh gross," Debbie said.

The smell of pizza was overpowering. We tore open the boxes. There were two large pizzas, pepperoni and mushroom and pineapple and ham. In the bag with the pop and cupcake there was a scrap of paper with the words, 'Happy Birthday' printed in pencil.

"It could only be from Nosh," Lauren said.

"Oh," Debbie said. "That's sweet." She sniffed back a tear and was silent for a moment. Then she looked up and smiled. "Will you share it with me?"

"Sure," I said. The others nodded. What a rotten way to spend a birthday, I thought, but

Debbie was holding up fine.

In between bites of pizza, we compared notes. We all had pretty much the same description of the room where Melvin was sitting.

"Did anyone get a look at the floors below as the elevator passed them?" I asked.

"It was pretty dark," Spazz said. "I'm not sure, but I think the floor below us has a door leading off the room. The entrance to the third floor looks like it's mostly boarded up. I didn't notice anything special about the second."

"I noticed the third floor was boarded up all right," I said. "There were no beds in the room where Melvin was so they must sleep somewhere else. Anything else?"

Lauren shook her head.

"I stood on the toilet seat and looked out the little window," Debbie said. "It had bars on the outside — no way out there. I think I could see a railway track outside, but it didn't look like it was used much. There was another old brick building across the track but I couldn't see any name on it."

"Where do you think we are?" I asked. We'd finished all the pizza and Debbie had insisted we all have a bite of her cupcake but none of us felt like singing Happy Birthday.

"I think we must be in one of the old warehouse districts in the city," Lauren said. "The rail line kinda confirms that. We were heading east before they blindfolded us, but they could have changed direction. I doubt if they headed back in the opposite direction though, they'd run the risk of hitting rush hour traffic and the police. Wait a minute. Let's have a look at the pizza boxes." Lauren took one of the pizza boxes and stood under one of the windows. We followed. There was just enough light to make out the name, Pizza King.

"I think there are four locations listed on the box," Lauren said. "It's hard to read them, it's too dark. I know there's one right downtown, so that can't be it. I think I can just make out the addresses. One is on Lavender Street, North. There's a few old warehouses in that area. My guess is that we're on the north end of the city. The pizza was really warm and the pop was cold, so whoever brought it here probably didn't come far."

"You're probably right, Lauren," I said. "But our main problem, I think, is to convince these dummies that Spazz isn't Billy T. If we can do that, they'll realize it's no use holding us."

"But we've been through all that," Lauren said. "It didn't work."

"Oh well," Debbie said. "Let's make ourselves as comfortable as possible. I need a blanket. I'm getting cold. Then we'll make a comparison between Spazz and Billy T. Hey! What's that?"

The sound of music drifted up the elevator

shaft.

"Must be a radio. Melvin was listening to one," I said.

"It doesn't sound like a radio, more like live music," Spazz said.

"So maybe they want to entertain us," Lauren said. "Who cares? Let's get comfortable."

We collected the blankets, covered ourselves and settled down against the wall. Spazz and I were the only ones with jackets and the girls gratefully accepted them as pillows.

When we were settled, Debbie asked, "Now, what are the differences? Spazz, tell us everything you know about Billy T. You must know lots about him."

"Only what I've read in magazines. But, okay. I'll try to think of everything I know. I think they'll realize I'm not Billy T tomorrow anyway. Glory said she's gonna have me phone my — his — agent tomorrow and have him come up with the ransom."

"You know who Billy T's agent is?" Lauren asked.

"Yeah, his agent is John de Marco. He's in New York. I don't know his phone number but I'll bet Glory does. She seems to be the brains behind all this."

"Yeah. I think you're right," I said. "She said something in the car about Melvin and Nosh screwing up before, so maybe this isn't the first time they've tried something like this."

"We're wasting time," Debbie said. "Let Spazz tell us everything he knows about Billy T and see if it will help."

Spazz did. He knew a lot. "He's four years older than me," he began. "He was born Billy Becker in New York City. The Bronx. His mother was Jewish, his father Catholic, but he was brought up in the Jewish faith, at least when he was young. His birthday is November fourth. He's a Scorpio. His father was a small-time watchmaker. You want to hear about his musical career?"

"Yes, everything," Debbie said. "You never know what might be useful."

Spazz continued. He knew every one of Black Vulture's hits, even the lyrics. It took about an hour before he finally stopped.

"Phew, Spazz, do you memorize all that stuff or what?" Lauren asked.

"No. I'm just a fan. I know lots about other groups too."

"Well I'm a fan too, but I never knew half of that."

"I think the fact that Spazz knows so much only makes things worse," I said. "If they gave him a quiz on Billy T, he'd get a hundred per cent."

"He could lie," Lauren retorted.

"Well, short of persuading Glory to bring in an electric guitar and have Spazz sing," I said,

"I don't know what to suggest."

"She'd never believe that anyway. He could be pretending he didn't have any talent," Lauren said.

"I was only kidding," I said.

"I'll have you know, Lauren," Spazz said, chuckling, "I may be very talented. You ever want to come over to my place and get in the shower with me, I'll sing my head off."

"Thanks, but no thanks," Lauren said.

"Get serious, you guys," Debbie said. "Be quiet and think. Think about all the stuff Spazz said."

Everyone shut up then. We lay there for quite a while without saying anything and despite the hard floor, I almost dozed off.

"Spazz," Debbie said suddenly. "You don't have a New York accent. You said Billy T came from New York."

"No good, Debbie," Spazz said. "Billy moved around so much, he doesn't talk much different than me now."

"There must be something we can use." Debbie lapsed into silence again. "Wait a minute. You know you said that Billy T was Jewish."

"Yeah?"

"Well if he was Jewish, wouldn't he be, you know …"

"What?" Spazz asked.

"Oh. This is so embarrassing," Debbie went

on. "Thank God it's dark, I can feel myself blushing. Well what I mean is ... If Billy T was Jewish, wouldn't he be ... You know ... circumcised? There I've said it."

"So?" Spazz asked.

I nearly choked and I could feel Lauren shaking with silent laughter beside me.

"Well?" Debbie questioned. "Oh, Spazz. You're making this so difficult." She sighed. "Are you?"

"What? Jewish?"

"No, Spazz you dope, circumcised for Pete's sake?"

I couldn't control myself any longer and neither could Lauren. We both broke out into fits of laughter.

"Oh shut up you two," Debbie said. "This is serious. Well? Spazz? What's the answer?"

"Sorry to disappoint you, but yeah, I am." He sounded miffed.

"Oh," Debbie said. "Too bad."

"I'm sorry," Spazz said.

Lauren and I continued to roll with laughter on the floor.

"It's not your fault," Debbie muttered.

"I know that," Spazz said. "I'm sure if when I was born my parents had known I was going to be kidnapped, they'd never have agreed to let the doctor do that to me."

"Forget it, Spazz," Debbie said in an embarrassed voice. "It was just an idea."

"Yeah? And if I wasn't, what did you expect me to do? Go to Glory with her pointing a gun at me and say, Hey! Glory. I'm not Billy T. Here's the proof. Holy!"

"Forget it, Spazz," Debbie snapped. "You don't have to. Go to sleep."

I thought, as I shook with laughter, that I'd better stop. Laughing so hard would only make me want to go. And there was no way I wanted to get up and use that pail even if it was dark. But the more I tried to stop, the more I laughed. Lauren couldn't stop either and soon Debbie and Spazz joined in. It was probably a good thing for all of us to have a good laugh. Below us, the music seemed softer now and it sounded like someone was singing.

TEN

I was the first to wake up. I thought it was early, judging from the amount of light coming in the windows. My left hip hurt from lying on the hard floor. I sat up and looked at the others. Lauren was on my right, breathing softly, her blanket covering most of her head. Debbie was next to her. She looked even more beautiful, sleeping. I marvelled at her long dark lashes. Spazz was on my left, snoring quietly. He'd taken his Billy T wig off and rolled it up to make a pillow.

I felt cold and I wanted to go to the bathroom. I lay down again and rolled over on my right hip and tried to go back to sleep but it was hopeless. I hoped Glory and her gang weren't late sleepers otherwise I'd be forced to use the pail.

Debbie stirred. Her eyes fluttered open and she saw I was awake. She stretched and stifled a yawn. I noticed the watch on her wrist.

"What time is it?" I whispered.

"Seven twenty-five," she whispered back. "Oh, I ache all over. This floor is awful hard. I need to go to the bathroom, but I'm not using that pail."

"Me too," I whispered.

"I'm sorry. I'll wake the others but I'm not gonna wait any longer." She got up and went to the edge of the elevator shaft. She lay down at the edge. "Hey! You down there. We need to go to the bathroom," she yelled. "Hey! Hey! You hear me?"

"What's goin' on?" Spazz sat up.

Lauren moaned, pulled the blanket off her head and opened her eyes. She closed them again but they flew open when Debbie started yelling again.

"We have to use the bathroom! You down there, let us down!"

There was no sound from below.

"Hey!" Debbie yelled again. She sounded really mad.

She got to her feet, walked over to the pail. I thought she was going to use it. Lauren jumped up with her blanket, I think with the idea of using it as a screen, but Debbie picked up the pail, brushed past Lauren and hurled it down the elevator shaft.

There were a couple of crashes, then a loud clang. I figured the pail must have bounced off the sides of the shaft then landed on top of the elevator.

"That was dumb," Lauren said. "Now what do we use?"

"You can use that elevator shaft if you want for all I care," Debbie snapped. "But I want the bathroom."

There was a whir from below. The elevator was coming up.

We waited in silence. When it appeared above the edge of the floor, we saw that the pail was standing upright on top of the elevator. Nosh was the elevator's only passenger and he looked worried. There was a slight crunching sound as the elevator jerked to a stop. Nosh didn't open the door.

"Melvin is mad," he said. "You woke him up. Glory too. I said I would come up and check. Glory said I could come up and see but I wasn't to open the door."

Debbie smiled at Nosh. "Thanks for the cake last night, Nosh. It was your idea, wasn't it?"

Nosh grinned sheepishly. "Yeah. I wanted to send a candle but I didn't have one."

"That was very kind of you. Look, Nosh. I have to go to the bathroom. So do the others. You can take us down one by one. We promise we won't try to escape."

Nosh looked uncertain. "You promise?"

"I promise." She turned to us. "We all do, don't we."

We mumbled, "Yeah." Right then I'd have promised anything. I needed to go so desperately.

"Okay," Nosh said. "No tricks now."

He opened the elevator door just wide enough to allow Debbie to step in. He closed it quickly behind her and started the elevator down. As the roof of the elevator passed, I noticed that the pail on top was badly dented.

"Where does she get off, promising that we won't try to escape?" Lauren asked.

"It got her the use of the bathroom," I said. "Something I need badly too. Anyway, this is another chance for us to take another look around. Let's see if we can learn anything that will help us."

It seemed to take ages for Debbie and Nosh to return.

It was agreed I should go next, because I seemed to have the greatest need.

I studied the floors we passed on the way down. Spazz was partly right. The floor below us had two doors off it, not one, but I had no idea where they led. The room looked smaller and completely empty. The third floor had planks nailed across the opening and, as we went past, I noticed that part of the ceiling had fallen down. The floor was covered in chunks of plaster. The second floor room was empty, but it had two doors leading off it too.

When the elevator reached the main floor, I saw that Glory was waiting. She held a gun in her hand. "You can have a wash up in the sink if you want, but make it quick." She threw me a towel.

Nosh followed me to the bathroom and waited outside. The sink was outside the door. After using the toilet, I stood on the seat and confirmed what Debbie had described. I went out, took off my shirt and splashed water on myself. There was a small bar of soap. Nosh stood in the hall watching me as I washed. Glory took the towel from me when I went back. Spazz went next.

"I got Glory to agree to let us use the toilet and let us wash," Debbie said. "She says we can use it twice before noon and twice in the afternoon. She said as long as we behave, it's okay. But any tricks, and she'll give us another pail and we won't be allowed down at all."

As Spazz returned and Lauren went down with Nosh, we heard a car drive off. "Melvin is going to get us some breakfast," Spazz said. "In an hour, they're gonna take me to a phone to call Billy's agent. I think Glory's gonna do most of the talking. She said she'd put me on the phone for just a minute so Billy's agent will know I'm Billy. That's when I hope she'll realize I'm not Billy and let us go. I tried to persuade her to let you guys all go now, but she says they have to keep you here until the money is turned over. I don't know how she plans to get the money."

Lauren returned and again we compared notes. We hadn't found out much more. There was the sound of the returning vehicle and, a few minutes later, Nosh brought up our breakfasts. There were four Egg McMuffins and coffee from McDonalds. Although we checked the container, there was no address listed on it.

As soon as we finished eating, Lauren said, "You know, we could probably reach a window if we formed a sort of pyramid. Kevin, if you and Spazz could kneel down maybe I could take Debbie on my shoulders and stand on your backs. She might be just about able to see over the edge of the window."

"It's worth a try," Debbie said. "Do you think you can support me?"

"You're not much heavier than I am, but you're a bit taller and your arms are longer," Lauren said. "Maybe you could reach up and pull yourself up a bit."

"Okay."

Spazz and I got down on all fours, side by side under one of the windows. Lauren ducked under Debbie and managed to get her onto her shoulders. She staggered a bit.

"Lower your backs a bit, you guys," she said. "It's too high a step."

We did and she managed to step up. I felt her wobble as Spazz and I raised our backs again.

"Can you see anything, Debbie?" Lauren asked. Her voice sounded a bit strained like she was having trouble keeping Debbie up.

"Just a sec," Debbie said. "My eyes are just about level with the window. I'm gonna pull myself up a bit, hang on."

I felt Lauren's foot shift on my shoulders, then Debbie said, "I can just see the top of another building and, wait a minute, a water tower, I think on a building behind the first one. It has something written on it. I think it says, 'W-O-O-F-I-E'. Woofie. That's about all I can see."

I looked up over my shoulder. "That's the name of a dog food company," I said. Then, because I was looking straight up, I couldn't help adding, "Gee, you've got nice legs, Lauren."

"You jerk," Lauren said, and I felt her foot grind into the back of my neck.

That, combined with the fact that Spazz and I both started to laugh, caused our little pyramid to collapse. Lauren's foot slipped off my back and Debbie came down fast. Luckily, she managed to land on her feet.

"You guys," Lauren reprimanded us. "If we're gonna get out of here, you've gotta co-operate, not fool around."

"Sorry," I mumbled. "I ..."

The sound of the elevator rising stopped me from saying anything more.

It was Glory and Melvin.

"You," Glory pointed at Spazz. "Come on."

"Good luck, Spazz," I said.

"Thanks," he mumbled.

When he was gone, I took another look at the elevator shaft. The girls folded up the blankets and sat on them against the wall. They didn't say anything. They were too worried.

The elevator started up about fifteen minutes later. Glory and Melvin were with Spazz again and they didn't look too happy. We looked expectantly at Spazz. He shook his head.

"Well?" I demanded, when the elevator had gone. "What happened? Did Billy T's agent confirm you weren't him?"

"Not exactly." Spazz looked worried. "They took me in the car to a public phone booth just a couple of blocks away. You were right, Lauren. This is on the north end of the city. Most of the warehouses seem to be deserted. This one has 'Condemned' and 'Keep Out' signs on the outside. There was no one around. Melvin kept me covered the whole time. Glory made the call. She knew the number all right and she had lots of change ready just in case. She did most of the talking. She must have talked to de Marco's secretary first because she said, 'Billy T Banko calling for Mr. de Marco.' Then he must have come on the line because she said, 'We're holding Billy T Banko. We want to do a deal. We want two hundred thousand in cash by Monday morning. I'll tell you when and where. You control Billy T's money, so you get it together. We'll call you back in a couple of hours. Any tricks and Billy T has made his last recording.' Then she said, 'What do you mean, you just got off the phone to him, he's right here. I'll put him on.'

"She said to me," Spazz continued. "'Just read this. Don't say anything else.' She handed me a piece of paper and I had to say, 'I was kidnapped from The Ritz Plaza yesterday. Do as they say, John.' Then Glory grabbed the phone back."

"I heard her say, 'This is no hoax, check all you want. Phone him up then, if you know where he is. You've got two hours.' Then she slammed the phone down. That's it. She still doesn't believe me. I think she was counting on my voice to convince de Marco. He obviously knows where Billy T is, if he phoned him. He won't do anything about getting any money. He knows I'm not Billy T. I hope when Glory phones back next time, John de Marco will convince her she has the wrong guy."

The elevator was coming up again. Glory was the only one in it. She didn't bother to open the door. She just stuffed a newspaper through the grilled door and sent it skidding across the floor. "So! We've got the wrong guy have we? Read that!" she yelled triumphantly. Then she was gone.

Spazz picked up the newspaper. It was the Saturday morning *Chronicle*. We gathered round Spazz and looked over his shoulder.

I groaned when I saw a front page article that was headed, 'Girls Mob Ritz Plaza', and Spazz read aloud, "'Yesterday, hundreds of girls mobbed The Ritz Plaza when rumours spread that Billy T Banko, leader of the 'Heavy Metal' group Black Vulture, was staying at the hotel. Hotel security had to call in the police for assistance in clearing the hotel of the screaming fans, mostly young girls, who forced their way in in an attempt to meet the famous rocker. A spokesman for the hotel said that there was only some minor damage caused before police and hotel employees were able to oust the fans.

"The same spokesman declined to confirm or deny that Billy T was staying at the hotel stating that it was the hotel's policy never to disclose any information about its guests. Some patrons of the hotel's lobby restaurant, however, confirmed to the *Chronicle*'s reporter that they saw someone who matched Billy T's description being hustled out of the hotel under tight security. His current whereabouts are unknown, but there is no question that Billy T was in town yesterday. We refer our readers to page three for an exclusive interview with the elusive rock star by Jessica Kendall our entertainment reporter. Black Vulture's *Blondes at the Barricades* is the top selling album in the country at this time."

I groaned even louder when Spazz turned to page three. There was the interview all right. Glory had circled it with red pen. And, to make matters worse, there was the photograph of me and Spazz. The caption under the picture read, 'Billy T Banko and friend, Eric, at the 'French Underground' bistro yesterday.' The interview didn't say much. There was the bit about Billy T and Nirvana Nyx that Spazz had mentioned and the bit about Black Vulture's latest release. Jessica Kendall had added a few details of her own. But even though she had got my name wrong again, there was no denying it was me sitting beside Spazz. It was going to be even harder now to convince Glory and company that they'd got the wrong guy.

ELEVEN

"What do we do now?" Lauren asked. "If this de Marco guy doesn't convince Glory that Spazz isn't Billy T, we could be here for ages. De Marco won't get the money and they won't let us go until he does. What do you think they'll do with us? They won't just let us walk out of here, will they? We know too much about them. They wouldn't … You know … Would they …?" She sounded really worried.

We were all silent for a moment, thinking about what Lauren was thinking but had left unsaid.

"Naw," I said. "My guess is that as soon as they find out that Spazz is not really Billy T they'll hightail it out of here and just leave us behind."

"So what we should be doing is thinking

about ways to get out of here," Debbie said. "If they just leave us behind, it could be ages before anyone found us. We could starve to death. What if we just start hollering?"

"I don't think it would do any good," Spazz said. "When I was outside, there was no one even near this place. It's the weekend too, so anyone who works near here won't be around 'till Monday. And another thing, if we do kick up a racket, how long is it gonna be before they shut us up? Maybe gag us or tie us? Let's see what else we can come up with."

"One thing puzzles me," I said. "How come there is no mention in the paper of Lauren and Debbie being missing? Your parents must be going crazy by now."

Lauren sighed. "Not mine. I'm afraid I hinted that I was probably gonna spend the whole weekend with Carlene Deming, at her house. My mom isn't likely to phone Carlene's until late tomorrow night if I don't get home."

"Then, how come you were getting in such a flap about getting that maid's uniform back before your sister found out?" Spazz asked. "Won't your sister know it's missing?"

"No, she doesn't have to work until Tuesday night. Anyway she's gone away for the weekend."

"So what was the big deal about getting the uniform back?" Spazz persisted.

Lauren blushed. "I was embarrassed. I

found myself in the Royal Suite of The Ritz Plaza with two guys from Eastridge High, that's all."

"You didn't trust us, huh?" Spazz asked. "I don't get it, you wouldn't have been embarrassed if it had been Billy T in there instead of just Kevin and me?"

"Oh leave off, Spazz. The whole idea was dumb to begin with. Look, why am I explaining all this, anyway?"

"It's not important," Debbie said. "We've just got to think of a way out of here. Arguing about who did what doesn't help. I know my father will be worried sick. I disappeared right in the middle of my birthday party. To come back to Kevin's question about not being mentioned in the newspaper article, I think I read somewhere that the police don't consider you missing until after twenty-four hours. Daddy is sure to have gone to the police but they won't do anything official until after tonight."

"I think Debbie's right," I said. "So, do we just sit and wait or what?"

"Got any ideas?" Lauren asked. "I don't fancy spending another night in this place, never mind the whole weekend, but what do we do?"

"Well, I took another look at the elevator shaft," I said. "If I could get down to the next floor, maybe I could find some stairs. From what I could see, the floor below is much smaller than this. It has at least two doors leading off it. One of them must lead to some stairs, if they're not boarded up like the door here. It's worth a try."

"How would you get down there?" Lauren asked. "It's too dangerous and what if you fell?"

"Well, I'd need something like a rope or something we could make into a rope."

"All we have are these blankets," Spazz said. "If we tore them up, and they noticed, that would be the end of any escape plans. Anyway, if anyone is gonna climb down, it should be me. I'm the one who got us all into this."

"Let's have a look at the blankets anyway," I said. I picked one up and held it by the corner and tried to start a tear. I used all my strength, grunting with the effort, but the blanket wouldn't rip. Spazz and the girls tried too, but it was no use.

"These must be army blankets or something," I said. "I've never seen such heavy blankets."

"We either need a pair of sharp scissors or find a way of tying them together," Spazz said.

"I think it's too dangerous anyway," Lauren said. "We're all still alive and well. Why risk getting killed?"

The mention of getting killed made us all think for a minute. I had said that I didn't think the gang would harm us, but there was no guarantee. "Let's see if we can tie two blankets together," I said.

We found that was hopeless too. The blankets were too thick and wouldn't knot properly.

"We'll have to think of something else," I said. "What else have we got we can use?"

"There's these ties we bought." Spazz picked up his jacket and pulled out the package.

"Great," I said. "Let's have them."

When Lauren saw the ties she said, "Wow! You guys bought these?"

"Hey, these are hand-painted." Debbie ran her hand over them. "Expensive."

"I'll say," I said. "Ninety bucks each, but Billy T paid for them actually." As I was speaking I was knotting the ties together. "All right, Spazz, it's tug o' war time. Let's see how strong these things are."

Spazz and I sat on the floor opposite each other and pulled on the ties for all we were worth. They held.

"So much for that," I said. "Let's see how far they'll reach."

We all went to the elevator shaft and lay down on the floor. I dangled the ties over the edge.

"God, it's scary," Debbie said. "Look how far down it is. Forget it."

"The ties don't even reach half way," Spazz

said.

He was right. The end of the ties was at least six feet above where the opening to the fourth floor began. Even if I dangled from the last inch of tie, my feet wouldn't reach the opening. I hauled them up.

"I'm glad that's out," Lauren said. "It gives me the creeps looking down there."

"Me too," Debbie said.

"We need something else to knot onto the ties to make them longer, something strong."

"Like what?" Spazz asked.

"I dunno," I said. "Maybe a belt. Darn. I changed my jeans yesterday and left my belt on the other pair."

The designer pants Billy T had given Spazz didn't need a belt and Lauren's uniform and Debbie's dress didn't have one either.

"There is something you might use," Debbie said. "But no, forget it."

"What?" I asked.

"It's too dangerous. I don't want to be responsible for getting anyone killed."

"Tell us anyway," I said.

"No. Give up this crazy idea."

"So what is it?" Spazz urged.

"Don't laugh. It wouldn't work anyway," Debbie said. "It's crazy." She blushed. "Well, both Lauren and I are wearing pantyhose, and … Well … I've heard people use them in an emergency for fan belts on cars, so they must be fairly strong. That was my idea, it's stupid, I know. They'd probably rip."

"Maybe not," I said. "It can't do any harm to find out how strong they are anyway. Come on, girls, hand them over."

"No," Debbie said. "I don't want anything to go wrong."

"Look," I said. "Spazz and I will tie them together and pull like crazy. If they don't hold, we'll give up on the idea, okay? But even if we do forget about trying to climb down the shaft, a rope might come in handy in some other way later, like to rope up a couple of the gang or something. Maybe we can jump them when they come up in the elevator."

"Well..." Debbie sounded doubtful.

"It might be useful to have a rope like Kevin says," Lauren added. "It's best to be pre-pared."

"Okay," Debbie said. "You two guys turn your backs."

We did.

"Here," Lauren said. We turned around and the girls handed us the pantyhose.

"They're awful short," Spazz said.

"They stretch, dummy," Lauren said.

"Okay, Spazz," I said. "Ready for the tor-ture test?"

I had tied the pantyhose together and then onto the ties. Again Spazz and I went into our tug o' war routine.

The pantyhose stretched, but they held.

Lauren laughed. "My sister would die if she saw what you guys have done to her pantyhose."

"Strong stuff," I said. "Let's see if they reach."

"Oh no, don't," Debbie moaned. "I'm sorry I mentioned it."

"Let's just have a look," I said.

The pantyhose just gave enough added length to reach a little way past the opening and I figured I could get my hands on a little ledge just above the doorway and swing into the room.

Spazz and I then had an argument over who should go, but I settled *that* when I asked who was the best rope climber in the school and pointed out I was lighter. The girls wanted me to forget it but I ignored their protests.

I tied one end of the ties over an old metal hinge bracket just at the edge of the doorway and tested it by pulling on it. Then with Spazz holding onto me, I gingerly lowered myself over the edge.

Spazz released his grip on me as I went below his reach and all my weight was being taken by the ties. I hoped Billy T's money had been well spent.

I tried to find footholds along the side of the shaft but it was perfectly smooth. I glanced up once and saw the frightened faces of my three friends. Debbie was half covering her eyes with her hands. I tried to smile to give them reassurance but I'm sure all they saw was a grimace.

I reached the first pair of pantyhose and continued down. I felt them stretch alarmingly but they held. I knew they were the pair Lauren had been wearing. They were black to match her maid's outfit. If they give out now, I thought, these will be my last thoughts. They're stretching so much, they'll never fit Lauren's sister again, or anyone else for that matter.

I felt my feet touch the ledge and I knew I was just above the doorway. Just a few more feet and I could swing inside. Suddenly I heard a whirring sound below. I glanced down. I was horrified to see that the elevator was coming up.

I panicked for a second and I heard a small scream above me. What to do? Try to scramble the last few feet to the doorway below before the elevator got there or try to climb up? The elevator looked like it was coming fast. I started climbing madly in a frantic effort to get back up.

I was only half way up and I could see Spazz's outstretched hands waiting to grab me when the elevator hit me. It knocked the breath out of me and I found myself lying spread-eagled on top of it beside the metal pail that Debbie had thrown down. I thought, I'll jump off as soon as it reaches the edge of our floor. I tried to position myself to make a dive forward but something was wrong, I was tangled up in my makeshift rope.

In a frenzy I tried to untangle myself and realized at the last second that I was already passing our floor. I caught a flash of three white faces, one with a hand over a mouth and then I threw myself as flat as possible waiting to be crushed against the roof of the elevator shaft.

——— TWELVE ———

I wanted to scream but I didn't. There was a loud clunk beside my head and then a grinding noise. I felt pressure on one shoulder, and I thought, this is it. But it only lasted a second. I felt the elevator jerk and the pressure eased.

I realized that the elevator had stopped at our floor.

I couldn't raise my head because the roof of the shaft was only inches away, but I could move my arms. I struggled with the rope and somehow managed to get myself untangled. Then I heard voices.

I recognized Debbie's. "Oh thank you. That's awfully kind of you. I love it. But right now, I've got to go to the bathroom real bad. Hurry, please, let me come down with you." She sounded desperate, almost panic stricken.

"Well, all right." It was Nosh. He sounded puzzled. "No tricks now."

I heard the door open and I felt the elevator bounce. I guessed Debbie was inside. The door closed and the elevator started down.

This time I made no mistake. As soon as the room appeared, I launched myself into it. I crashed into Spazz and Lauren and sent them sprawling. They were, I found out later, ready to pull my crushed and broken body off the elevator as it went past. I felt something soft and squishy against my shirt and I thought I must be bleeding, but I didn't have time to check. Lauren was hugging me.

"Oh, thank God! You're alive!" She started to cry as she sat on the floor holding me.

"Good to see you, buddy." Spazz's voice shook as he spoke.

"Promise me you'll never do anything dumb like that again?" Lauren sobbed. Then she was kissing me.

"I dunno," I said grinning, when she stopped kissing me. "I think it was worth it."

We heard the elevator returning. This time Glory was with Nosh and Debbie, and Glory had her gun. The relief on Debbie's face when she saw me was really something, but she said nothing.

"What's goin' on?" Glory asked suspiciously. "Nosh here thinks one of you was missing."

"No there wasn't," Debbie said. "He just didn't see Kevin. He was sitting over in the corner, sulking. Nosh couldn't see him because he didn't step out the door of the elevator, that's all."

"Hmm," Glory said. "You dummy, Nosh."

"Sorry, Glory. I got confused."

"That's okay, Nosh. Anyway, it's about time for Billy to come down to help me make that phone call."

When Spazz left, Debbie turned to me. "Oh, Kevin. I was worried sick. I was sure you were killed. I almost told them downstairs. When Nosh came and brought me another cup cake all I could think of was you being crushed on top of that elevator. I whispered to Lauren that she and Spazz must try to grab you when it went down. I knew it would have to be fast. I didn't want Nosh finding out you were gone, but I didn't know what to do."

"I'm fine," I said. "That pail you threw on top of the elevator may have saved me. It gets scrunched a bit more every time the elevator comes up. I'm afraid your cup cake did too. I landed on it when I jumped off the elevator. I've got icing sugar all over my shirt, look."

"Oh, Kevin." Then it was Debbie's turn to hug me.

Melvin and Glory brought Spazz back a short while later. Spazz looked hopeful. Glory looked worried.

"John de Marco hung up on Glory," Spazz said, when the elevator had gone. "He figures it's a hoax. He insists that he knows exactly where Billy T is and he threatened to call the cops if Glory phones back again. Glory put me on for a sec and he told me to buzz off. Actually, he used stronger words than that. I worked on Glory on the way back and told her about Billy T getting married. She hasn't bought it yet, but I think maybe she's beginning to wonder. Especially since John de Marco doesn't give two hoots about me and won't come up with any money."

We spent the afternoon just sitting and talking, mostly about school. There wasn't anything else to talk about. We hadn't come up with any more escape plans. Glory and Nosh hadn't noticed our rope. It must have been caught up along a side wall of the elevator where it couldn't be seen and some of it got tangled up with me on the roof. I'd untied it as soon as Lauren had stopped kissing me and it was now hidden under the blankets.

We were eating the fish and chips Melvin had brought us for lunch. The outside wrapping was newspaper with a sticker that said Ye Olde English Fish And Chip Shoppe but there was no address to help us pinpoint our location this time, although we were sure our earlier guesses were right.

"Hey! Look at this," Lauren said. "This was

part of this afternoon's paper. Here's some more about Billy T."

We crowded round.

"Read it out," I said.

"The headline says, 'Billy T Seen in Martinique.' Where's that? Oh, it says here it's one of the French islands in the Caribbean."

"Well read it," I said impatiently.

"Hang on a sec. There's a lot of grease from the chips on it, it's hard to read. Okay, it says here that, 'It is rumoured that Billy T Banko got married by a justice of the peace in the town of Le Marin, Martinique, early this morning. No other details were available but sources say that a marriage licence was issued for a William Becker. William Becker is the birth name of Billy T Banko. There was no word on the name of the bride.' It's torn here, just a minute." Lauren scrabbled around in the remains of the newspaper wrappings.

"Ah, here's another bit." She continued reading, "'… was contacted in Atlanta where she is recording an album. The rock star had nothing more to add to the report except to say that she and Mr. Banko were no longer romantically involved. She went on to say that she believed it was highly likely that the marriage took place and offered Mr. Banko and his bride her congratulations if the rumour proved to be true.'"

"That's Nirvana Nyx in that bit," Spazz

said. "Is there any more?"

"Just a rehash of part of the story from this morning's paper. This is an early afternoon edition, it says at the top. Hey! We've got to show this to Glory. She's gotta believe us now. Come on let's get her up here. It's time for a bathroom break anyway."

Lauren went over to the elevator shaft and we all joined her and started yelling. A few minutes later, the elevator started up. Melvin was the only passenger.

"All right. What is it now? You're becoming real pests. I suppose you want to go to the bathroom."

"Yeah," Lauren said. "But, what's more important, take a look at this."

Melvin hadn't opened the door of the elevator and Lauren had to stuff the bits of newspaper through the door to him.

"What is this?"

"That was wrapped around the fish and chips you brought us. Read it."

"It proves that I'm not Billy T Banko," Spazz said. "It's this afternoon's paper."

"Yeah? Is this some kind of trick?" Melvin eyed the pieces of paper suspiciously but made no attempt to read them.

"Oh for heaven's sake!" Debbie said. "Just read it. What do you think we did? Printed it ourselves?"

"You." He pointed at Lauren. "You come

119

with me."

We were in high spirits while we waited for Lauren to return. We all felt that our ordeal would soon be over.

When she returned with Melvin, we crowded round her. "Well, does Glory believe us now?" Spazz asked.

"She says it's just a rumour right now. She's gonna wait until the late editions of the papers come out. She'll let us know then. Probably after supper."

"What's she waiting for?" Spazz asked. "How much more proof does she need? What did Melvin say?"

"He's goin' along with Glory. Whatever she says, goes. We'll just have to wait."

The hours seemed to drag by. The rest of us had our bathroom breaks and then Glory arrived with Melvin carrying our supper. It was pizza again. We could smell it.

"These guys don't go in for much variety, do they?" Debbie asked.

We all noticed the newspapers under Glory's arm right away. We waited expectantly. Melvin shoved the boxes of pizza across the floor at us.

Glory had a funny glint in her eye. She opened one of the newspapers. "Okay, listen up. I'm beginning to think we may have made a mistake with our friend here." She pointed to Spazz. "I'm not entirely convinced quite yet, but his agent doesn't want to pay any money for him anyway. But, with her!" Here Glory pointed to Debbie. "Maybe we've got a winner."

"What do you mean?" I asked.

"If you're convinced Spazz isn't really Billy T there's no reason to hold us. We told you we're just ordinary school kids," Lauren complained.

"I don't think so. Not her anyway. That's not what these papers say. What we have here is none other than the heiress to Spatz Vista Brewery."

Debbie gasped.

"Now her daddy," Glory went on, "should be able to come up with a little dough, don't you think? And if Billy here still pans out, well, maybe we've got ourselves the daily double. I'll talk to you later once I've had a chance to think. Enjoy your supper."

"Wait a minute," I said. "What are you talking about? What's she talking about, Debbie?"

Debbie wasn't saying anything. She had gone very still.

"Here," Glory said. "If you're all high school kids like you say, you can read these yourself. Here's your bedtime reading." She tossed the newspapers down on the floor, slammed the door of the elevator and she and Melvin left.

THIRTEEN

We all stared at Debbie.

"Is it true what Glory said?" Lauren asked. "I mean about your father owning Spatz Vista Brewery?"

Debbie nodded.

"But if you're all that rich why would you go to an ordinary school like Eastridge High?" Lauren went on. "I thought all rich kids went to private schools."

Debbie sank slowly to the floor and put her head in her hands. "That was my choice," she said quietly. "And I'm not that rich."

"But your dad does own Spatz Vista Brewery?" Spazz asked. "I never knew that."

"I haven't gone around broadcasting it. But then I don't know what any of your parents do either. Should I?"

"I guess not," Spazz mumbled.

"My daddy's not the only owner of the brewery," Debbie continued softly. "But he is the major shareholder. I don't consider myself to be a rich kid. I suppose we are well off, and I guess I could have gone to a private school. Daddy wanted me to. But I didn't want that. I like being at Eastridge High."

While Debbie was speaking, I picked up one of the newspapers. It was *The Daily Spectator*, a tabloid. A headline on the front page read, 'Daughter Of Local Brewery Owner Rumoured Missing.' There was a picture of Debbie, and underneath, a smaller headline asked, 'Is She Mystery Girl Who Wed Billy T Banko?'

I gasped and muttered, "Where do they get this stuff?"

Spazz and Lauren leaned over my shoulder to look.

"They've got your picture here in the paper!" Lauren exclaimed. "How did they get that?"

Debbie scrambled to her feet. "I don't know where they got it, but that's the picture from our junior high yearbook. Daddy would never have given them that, here, let me read it."

I handed the paper to Debbie.

Spazz had picked up the other newspaper.

"Oh my God! How could they write this?" Debbie gasped. "It says here that I may have run off to marry Billy T. A number of eyewitnesses, it says, saw me rush off from The Ritz Plaza with the rock star late Friday afternoon. What! Listen to this, 'Judith Finch, a close friend of the missing girl, told *The Spectator*, "We were celebrating Debbie's sixteenth birthday at the hotel when Billy T and his entourage swept through the lobby. One minute Debbie was there and the next she was in Billy T Banko's arms. I didn't even know she was a fan of his. I've heard of love at first sight and all that, but if you ask me, I think she and Billy T had it all planned."

"How could she say that! Had it all planned! A close friend of mine, it says. Hah. Not any more. What a ninny that Judith Finch is. Fink is more like it!" Debbie began tearing the newspaper to shreds.

"That is *The Daily Spectator*," I said. "You know how it makes up stories all the time, Judith probably didn't even say that."

"*The Chronicle* doesn't go that far," Spazz said. "It simply says you may have disappeared but police would neither confirm nor deny that. It says, '...the seventeen-year-old daughter...'" Spazz paused. "I thought you were sixteen, not seventeen —"

"I am sixteen," Debbie snapped. "Don't these dumb newspapers get anything right?"

"'The seventeen-year-old daughter," Spazz continued, "of the owner of Spatz Vista Brewery may have left a birthday party, Friday, at The Ritz Plaza, with Billy T Banko, leader of the heavy metal group Black Vulture. *The Chronicle* reported in an earlier edition that it had it on good authority that the rock star was married early this morning on the French island of Martinique. *The Chronicle* has been unable to confirm this and so far has not been able to contact Mr. Carl Dobrazynski, the girl's father. Mr. Dobrazynski and Debbie's mother are divorced."

"Do they have to tell everything?" Debbie fumed.

"Take it easy, Debbie," I said. I could see she was really worked up.

"Take it easy! A few minutes ago we were getting out of here. We'd proven Spazz wasn't Billy T and now it's me they want money for. Take it easy! I'm sorry. Poor Daddy."

"Hey, it's okay, Debbie," Lauren said. "We're all in this together. We'll find a way out."

"Yeah." Spazz grinned. "At least you can prove you weren't circumcised."

That broke everyone up. "Oh Spazz, you jerk." Debbie hugged him as she joined in the laughter.

Below, the music started up. Spazz went over to the edge of the elevator shaft. "You know, that's not a radio or a tape on a ghetto blaster. Listen. I think that's Glory singing."

The rest of us followed Spazz and listened. A woman's clear voice could be heard coming up the shaft singing to the accompaniment of instruments.

"Hey, she's good, really good," Spazz said, "and whoever's playing that keyboard knows what they're doing."

We listened. Spazz was right. The song Glory was singing, if it was Glory, sounded terrific. The music had a real beat to it. The kind that makes you want to get up and dance.

"What's that song? You know it, Spazz?" Lauren asked.

"I dunno. I never heard it before."

The music stopped. There was a pause and it started over. The woman picked up the song again. Again the singer broke off and the music faded, then started again.

"It's like they're practicing," Spazz said.

"Hey," I said. "It's great entertainment, but what's our next move? Glory said she'd talk to us later when she had a chance to think. I guess she meant when she decides what their next move is. We should try to figure out what it will be and what we can do."

"Kevin's right," Lauren said. "What do you think they'll do, Kevin?"

"I'm not sure. But I think they might phone up Debbie's dad and tell him they have Debbie and ask for some money. He'll believe them, not like with Billy T's agent and Spazz. Debbie's dad knows she's missing, I doubt if he bought the story about Debbie running off with Billy T to get married."

Debbie snorted. "I don't know anyone who'd believe that, except maybe Judith Finch."

"Or the police," Lauren said. "They even helped our kidnappers get away. They'll be too embarrassed to admit that, so maybe they'd like to believe you ran off with Billy."

"Our kidnappers won't be able to phone Daddy though," Debbie murmured. "We have an unlisted number."

"They could send a note to your house, if they found out where you live," I said. "Or just drop one off at one of the newspapers or radio stations."

"If they send a note, it could be ages before anything happens," Lauren said. "Are we gonna just sit around and wait?"

"I don't want anyone climbing down that elevator shaft," Debbie said. "Not on my account, anyway. It's too dangerous."

"Maybe we could jump Nosh or something if he comes up by himself," Lauren suggested. "He likes Debbie. Maybe she could lure him out of the elevator. We could knock him out and get in the elevator."

"Yeah?" Spazz asked. "What then? Go down and find Melvin and Glory waiting for us with their guns?"

The music below had changed to a different beat and Glory's voice came up the shaft singing something slower.

We sat on the floor, thinking, but I found myself listening to the words of the song and Glory's sweet voice. I think everyone else was listening too.

Playing it cool's the way to be
When everything turns out wrong
Playin' it cool, playin' it cool
Playin' it cool's my song

Getting uptight
Will make nothin' right
Or get me through another day
And when people bad mouth you
I'll never doubt you
Yes I'm playin' it cool my way

Oh I may be a fool
But I'm playin' it cool
Yes I'm playin it cool my way.

"She sings beautifully," Lauren said as the song came to an end.

"It's a great song too," Spazz said. "I wonder whose hit it is? Anyone ever hear it before?"

The rest of us shook our heads. The next song was slow, about an old man at a beach trying to recall his youth. We listened, all thoughts of plans for escape gone out of our heads. We were somehow caught up in the music and Glory's voice as she sang,

Little children building
Crowded castles in the sand
With bottle caps and paper wraps
From near the hot dog stand
And on their coloured beach towels
All beautiful and tanned
The lovers and the lonely
await the promised land.
That's promised on their radios
For the old there's nothing planned

And standing underneath the trees
an old man with his memories
with his eyes he never sees
As he gazes at the shore
Where many many years before
He ran the one and only store
He still remembers well.
The old man from the run-down beach motel

It's summer on the beach again
But it will never be the same
And the crazy flashing neon signs
Confuse an old man's sense of time
And the quiet places of the mind
Become a mad bazaar.

The music faded out.

"Someone's coming," I said.

We listened to the sound of the elevator coming up.

When it arrived it contained Glory and Nosh.

Glory slid back the door. "We couldn't get your phone number, Debbie. It's unlisted. Sorry, but you'll have to come with us and phone."

"Was that you singing, Glory?" Spazz asked.

"Yeah." Glory looked embarrassed. "You like it?"

"You sounded great," Spazz said.

"Thanks. Too bad those record companies out there don't think so. But singing and playing with the guys helps me think straight. Maybe if we get some dough out of this caper, Nosh, Melvin and me will make it out to Los Angeles and start over, give it another shot."

"Who's the keyboard player?" Spazz asked.

I thought, what's Spazz doing? Playing for time or what?

"Nosh, here," Glory answered. "He's my main man. Nosh may not be too swift at other things but he can play." Nosh hung his head, blushing furiously. "Melvin's our bass guitar player. But enough talk. Come on Debbie."

Debbie stepped into the elevator and Glory

closed the door behind her.

When the elevator had left, I turned to Spazz. "What was that all about, Spazz? You got something in mind?"

"No," Spazz said. "I was just interested in the music, that's all. They're great."

"I thought for a minute you were stalling or something. Getting ready to jump Nosh and Glory."

"No. Sorry."

I might have known Spazz would only have been thinking about the music.

We waited. It seemed like a long time before they brought Debbie back.

"What happened?" Lauren asked.

"At first, I thought about refusing to phone," she said. "But I knew Daddy would be worried. I dialled the number and as soon as I did, Glory grabbed the phone."

"She said, 'We have your daughter, Debbie, Mr. Dobrazynski. Don't worry she's fine. We won't hurt her.' Then Daddy must have asked Glory to prove I was okay because Glory put me on the phone. I tried to give him some clue to where we are. I couldn't say much though, with Glory standing there listening."

"What did you say?" Lauren asked.

"I told him I was okay. I hadn't been harmed."

"Yeah but what's the clue in that?" Lauren asked.

"Oh. I called him Woofie."

"Woofie?" Spazz repeated.

"Yeah, the name of the dog food company."

"You call your dad after a dog food?" Spazz looked incredulous.

"Knock it off, Spazz," Lauren said. "Don't be such a dope. Let Debbie tell it."

"Well, I said something like, Oh, Woofie it's me, Debbie. I'm okay, I'm fine. They're treating me good. I love you, Woofie." Then Glory grabbed the phone back. She asked Daddy to get fifty thousand dollars together and she'd call back later. Then she hung up."

"Hmm. They wanted two hundred thousand for me," Spazz said.

"Oh, shut up, Spazz," Lauren said.

"That's great, Debbie," I said. "Did your dad say anything when you called him Woofie?"

"No. But he'll wonder why I called him that. He's sure to know it's a clue. Glory asked me about it though. She said, 'What's with this Woofie?' I told her it was a pet name for my daddy. I think she bought it, I'm not sure. Unless she realizes that that dog food place is just a block away."

"Oh. I get it," Spazz said, grinning.

"Yea, Spazz," Lauren and I said in unison.

"But if they catch on and realize what you've done they could panic," Lauren said. "If they think the police are gonna come around here, they may not wait. They could move us."

"Or there could be a shoot-out," Spazz said.

"Oh, no," Debbie said.

"We can only wait and see," I said. "Or, we could come up with another plan."

"Like what?" Lauren asked.

"Well, it's a bit risky," I said. "It's all a matter of timing."

"What is?" Debbie asked.

"Well, remember how I jumped off the elevator into this room."

"Oh no, not that again," Debbie said.

"Wait," I said. "I'm not suggesting we climb down the shaft. I'm thinking we might all be able to jump on top of the elevator when it starts down and jump off again when it gets opposite the floor below. Like I said, it's a matter of timing. The tricky part would be jumping off together before the elevator passed the opening."

"It's too dangerous," Debbie said. "I had this awful vision of you being smushed between the top of the elevator and the roof. You were lucky. There was just enough room for you but with four of us ..."

"We'd jump on only as it's going down and jump off together at the floor below. Then we'd check out the doors, find the stairs and sneak out. The chances are they won't have gone to the trouble of boarding up every door. Once we'd got to the floor below we'd wait until we thought they were asleep before sneaking down the stairs."

"What if we timed it wrong?" Lauren asked. "Jumped too late or too soon when we get to the fourth floor? I don't fancy smashing my face against the top of a door frame or the side of the shaft."

"We could practice," I said. "Look. If we all linked arms and counted, we can practice jumping. Let's try it."

We did. We linked ourselves together in a row with our arms across each other's backs.

"On the count of three," I said. "Pretend that the elevator has just gone below the level of our floor."

"One two three." We jumped together across the floor.

"Now everyone let go fast, turn around and link up again. Not bad," I said. "Let's try it again."

We practiced several times.

"The key would be to make sure we didn't jump too soon or they'd see us," Lauren said. "The top of the elevator would have to have reached the floor here before we jumped."

"We couldn't jump too late, either," Spazz said. "Or we'd come crashing down on the elevator and lose our balance and probably not be fast enough turning around to be ready to jump off at the fourth floor opening."

"Like I said," I repeated. "It's a matter of

timing. We'd have to keep our heads down too when we jumped off. What do you guys think? They still have to give us our bathroom breaks, we could try it when they bring the last person back."

"I dunno," Debbie said. "It seems awful dangerous. That pail might be in the way too. We could wait and see if the police come, if Daddy passes on the clue."

"Or wait until Glory figures it out herself and decides to move us someplace else, or we get caught up in a gun fight," Lauren said. "I'm not so sure about those cops shooting straight. Let's practice some more."

"They might know we'd jumped on," Spazz said. "They might hear us, or our weight coming onto the elevator might make it bump."

"Could be," I said. "Let's practice some more anyway. I can't think of a better excuse to get my arms around two beautiful girls."

FOURTEEN

We'd decided to give it a try.

I was the last to be taken down to go to the bathroom. Each time Glory and Nosh had arrived in the elevator they'd found the remaining three of us standing in a row close to the elevator with our arms around each other. To Glory and Nosh, it must have looked like there was a bond of solidarity between us or we couldn't wait to go to the bathroom.

What we were doing of course, was timing practice jumps every time the elevator went down. I thought we were getting pretty good at it, but I'm sure we all had guilty looks on our faces each time the elevator arrived.

When it was my turn to go down, I paid particular attention to the way the elevator was operated. Glory pulled on a lever which seemed to control only the stopping and starting but not the speed. At the bottom, we stopped a few inches above the level of the main floor and Glory jiggled the lever to line the elevator up with the floor.

Melvin was sitting on a chair quietly playing chords on a guitar. He looked very content. He glanced up and smiled as I passed on my way to the bathroom. A small keyboard was on the table and another guitar rested against the other chair. Although I wanted to take my time in the bathroom and go over every move we were going to have to make, I didn't dare take too long. I knew the longer I took, the more anxious and nervous the others would become. But it was me who had to get off the elevator and get in position again to make the jump. If I was too slow we couldn't make it.

On the way back up, I tried to judge how fast the elevator was going. How long did we have as it passed the openings to the other floors, particularly the fourth. It didn't seem like it was going that fast, but fast enough if we didn't time things right.

Glory seemed preoccupied both going down and coming back up. She looked worried. She said nothing. Nosh was humming happily to himself. As we passed the fourth floor opening, my heart was pounding. As soon as Glory opened the door, I would have to step out quickly, join the others and wait until Glory closed the door again and started down.

We reached our floor. The others were still there, their arms linked together, but they were closer to the elevator and they were doing some kind of dance. Lauren was chanting, "We do the hokey-pokey and we turn around ..." They stopped jigging when I arrived. I figured they were trying to look as natural as possible like they were just amusing themselves.

Glory opened the door and I walked the couple of steps to the others. I turned and faced the elevator. I grinned and said, "What's this hokey-pokey stuff? How do you do it anyway?" I wrapped my right arm across Lauren's back and we were all linked together. Debbie was next to Lauren, and Spazz was at the other end. Spazz had our makeshift rope stuffed inside his jacket in case we needed it later.

I kept my eye on the elevator door waiting for Glory to close it and start down. But she didn't. Not right away anyway. She had her hand on the door like she was about to slide it closed but she just stood there. She started to say something, stopped, then closed the door. She looked like she was going to speak, but changed her mind again. She pulled on the lever and the elevator started down. Nosh smiled and waved as the elevator left.

We edged closer to the elevator shaft and waited breathlessly as the elevator went down.

It seemed to be moving slower for some reason but I was probably wrong. As the top of it came almost level with the floor, I whispered, "Ready? Quietly. Now!"

We jumped.

I heard one of the girls gasp, but our timing was perfect. Our practicing had paid off. We teetered for a moment as we let go of each other, turned quickly around and then we were linked up again. With the wall of the shaft so close and flashing past, it seemed like the elevator was going at a terrific rate. I glanced to my left. Everyone was crouched over like we'd practiced, keeping their heads well down and ready for the leap forward when the fourth floor opening was large enough in front of us. The top of the opening appeared and I was sure I could feel everyone tense up, ready to spring forward.

Then there was a jerk and we were shaken around a bit. The elevator had come to a sudden stop. I looked into the frightened eyes of my friends. We'd stopped with only a couple of feet of the fourth floor opening showing. There was no way we could try jumping through the gap. If the elevator moved while we were attempting it, we'd be crushed between the elevator and the frame of the opening. And, if we did manage to scramble through, we'd be in full view of Glory and Nosh.

We waited for what seemed like ages. Then slowly the elevator started moving. It was going up.

Beside me, Lauren glanced up in horror at the approaching roof of the shaft and I heard her murmur, "Oh God."

"Everyone keep their head down," I whispered desperately. "Get ready to jump off at our floor again."

In a moment, it seemed, we were there. I could feel the urge to jump too quickly, before the top of the elevator actually reached the opening. This would be dangerous. If one of us tripped, we would all fall and be crushed before we could get up again. But we couldn't leave it too late either. Jumping too early or jumping too late would end in the same result.

We couldn't wait any longer. "Now," I gasped. We jumped and at the same time the elevator stopped. We came down in a tangled heap on the floor.

As we picked ourselves up, Glory inched the elevator up until it was level with the floor.

She and Nosh stared at us through the door but she didn't open it. "Are you all right?" Glory asked, and I could hear the concern in her voice. "I thought you were on top of the elevator, but I wasn't sure. I was afraid you'd be squashed on top of it. That's why I stopped it before it reached the top. Please don't do that again. You won't have to anyway. I've decided to let you go."

"You have?" Debbie gasped with relief.

"All of us?" I asked.

"Yeah. All of you. I was going to tell you just as I started down, but I decided to tell Melvin first. Then you jumped on top of the elevator. We felt a bump. I had to bring you back up. I didn't want you trying to escape and getting hurt."

"What made you decide to let us go?" Spazz asked.

"Because it's not right. I thought when you were Billy T we could get some money and no harm would be done. A few thousand is nothing to Billy T. His last record grossed two million and his latest is expected to make five. But when you turned out to be just an ordinary kid, everything changed. Then Debbie here turned out to be rich and I thought maybe there was still a chance for our dream to come true. But it's wrong, it won't work. Look, please wait until I can get Melvin. I'll bring him back and we'll talk. Promise me you won't try jumping on the elevator again."

"Okay," I said. "We promise." The others nodded.

"We'll be right back." Glory said. She and Nosh disappeared as Glory took the elevator down.

"Do you think it's a trick?" Lauren asked. "Are they really gonna let us go? Maybe they're just gonna take off and leave us."

"Either way," I said, "we'll be free soon. Even if they do take off, someone will find us by Monday. We can make a lot of noise and attract someone's attention."

"I'm not sure I trust them," Lauren said. "I bet they won't come back, or it's just a trick to give them more time to pick up the money from Debbie's dad."

"Well you're wrong on one count," Spazz said. "The elevator's on it's way up."

Melvin, Nosh and Glory were in it. They all stepped out.

"We want to ask you a big favour," Glory said.

"Has Melvin agreed to let us go?" I asked.

"Yes, we're all agreed. We're sorry we put you through this."

"Why did you then?" Lauren snapped.

Glory seemed nervous. She bit her lip. "We have this dream. We've had it for a long time. We've never had much. We always had to scrimp and scrape. The only things we have that are worth anything are our instruments. When our parents died what held us together was our music. Our daddy was a street musician and he taught us to play."

"Then, Melvin and Nosh are your brothers?" Debbie asked.

"Yeah," Glory said. "Melvin is four years older than Nosh and Nosh is two years older than me. It was Melvin who raised Nosh and me when Mom and Dad died."

"So, you've had it tough," Lauren said.

"That doesn't give you any excuse to go around kidnapping people."

"We know that," Glory said. "We made a mistake. A big one."

"Look, we didn't mean you no harm," Melvin said. "Me and Nosh here wanted to help Glory out, that's all."

Nosh smiled, then hung his head.

"By sticking guns in people's faces? How do you think that made us feel?" Lauren asked angrily.

"They weren't real guns," Melvin said.

"Those were fake guns!" I gasped. "Sheesh. We could've escaped real easy."

"How did we know that?" Debbie retorted.

"We wouldn't have hurt you," Melvin said. "We just had to act a little mean to make you believe us."

"Well we did believe you," Debbie said.

"We were just gonna get Billy T and hold him for a couple of days," Melvin said "We'd get some money, then go to Los Angeles and get a new start."

"So why grab four of us?" Lauren sounded mad. "And dumping us blindfolded up here, we could have fallen down that shaft and been killed."

"We're not professional kidnappers, Lauren," Glory said. "We've never done anything like this before. We're not professional anything. Let's face it, we're failures. Failures at kidnapping, failures in music, failures in everything." A tear rolled down Glory's cheek.

"You said something in the car about Melvin and Nosh screwing up before," I said. "What did you mean by that?"

"Nothing really," Glory answered. "When I ask them to do something it doesn't always get done right. We've never broken the law before, never done anything criminal, if that's what you're thinking. We're just failures."

"You're certainly not failures in music," Spazz said, "You're great."

"Yeah, tell me about it," Glory sniffed. "We've sent out tape after tape, nobody listens. You have to have an agent to be noticed. Sometimes the tapes come back unopened, just marked, 'return to sender'."

"But those songs you were singing. Whose are they?" Spazz asked. "We've never heard them before."

"I wrote the words and some of the music," Glory replied. "Melvin and Nosh did a lot of the music too."

"That song," Spazz said. "The one about the old guy, that mentioned the promised land being promised on the radio — is getting to L. A. the promised land for you?"

"Yeah, sort of I guess, and maybe getting someone to listen to us."

"So how was kidnapping us gonna help?"

Lauren demanded.

"We thought maybe if we had a bit of money we could go out to the coast and maybe record at a real high class recording studio. We don't have that kind of money. Everything we've ever recorded we've done on our own. We've even used this old building as our recording studio. Melvin was able to hook up the power again."

"But you were asking two hundred thousand from Billy T's agent?" Spazz said, "Would you need that much?"

"No. We would have accepted much less, even a couple of thousand would have helped, but if we'd asked for say, five thousand dollars, who'd believe us? With five thousand we could pay our way to the coast, buy some new clothes, and have some left over for a couple of hours in one of those recording studios."

"But even if you did get recorded in a professional recording studio, there's no guarantee anyone would listen to, or recognize, your talent," Spazz said.

"I know," Glory said. "It was just a crazy dream." She lapsed into silence.

"So," I said. "What was this favour you were gonna ask us for?"

"Another crazy idea. I …We were hopin' maybe when we let you go, you'd give us a couple of hours before turnin' us in."

"You mean help you get away?" Lauren gasped.

"Well, sort of. Maybe we'd head west in Melvin's van. We have a bit of money for gas but that's all."

"How far do you think you'd get before the police picked you up?" I asked.

"Yeah," Lauren added. "Anyway there was nothing to stop you from just taking off and leaving us here. Why didn't you do that?"

"I suppose I felt, and Melvin and Nosh agreed," Glory said, "that we should tell you we're sorry. It was my idea to grab Billy T but sometimes I do things that are a little crazy. So, we thought we should explain, that's all."

"I get it," Lauren said, "You're hoping that when you do get caught we'll have to say you apologized and you'll all get a lighter sentence."

"No," Glory said. "That's not what I thought at all. We just wanted to say we're sorry." More tears rolled down her cheeks and Nosh put his arm around her to comfort her.

I turned to the others. "What about it you guys?"

"What?" Lauren asked.

I turned to Melvin. Nosh was still comforting Glory. "Just give us a minute." I led our group away so we could talk in private.

"So, what?" Lauren asked again.

"Well, what about staying quiet for a couple

of hours to give them a chance to get away."

"After all we've been through?" Lauren exclaimed angrily. She seemed ready to explode but she lowered her voice. "Scaring the heck out of us, blindfolding us, ripping Debbie's slip, not to mention my sister's pantyhose."

I grinned. "Your sister's pantyhose isn't ripped," I said. "It's just stretched a little. Our captors had nothing to do with that. I did it. You can pick up a new pair on the way home. Besides, they don't really need our permission. They can just leave. If they take the elevator down now, we're probably stuck here until at least daylight."

"Debbie's dad will have the cops searching the whole country for them," Lauren said. "They're gonna get caught anyway."

"Maybe," I said.

"It'd be too bad to let talent like that go to jail," Spazz said.

"What? You mean we should let them escape, even help them?" Lauren's mouth dropped open.

My voice dropped to a whisper. "Look at it this way. No one knows that Spazz, me or you are even missing. The only one who is officially missing is Debbie. Her father knows. He's expecting a phone call back. If Debbie is free when she makes that phone call the kidnapping is over."

"But not the crime," Lauren said.

"I'm in favour of letting them go," Debbie said. "I don't want to see Glory and Nosh in jail, Melvin either. He only acted tough because he had to. If I can phone my father and tell him I'm okay, we can wait and give them a chance to get away."

"You're serious, Debbie?" Lauren asked.

"Yes, I am. I really don't think it will serve any purpose to put them in jail. They made a mistake. I think they deserve a second chance."

"You mean you want them to get clean away?" Lauren gasped.

"Yes, I do."

"Sheesh," Lauren said. "I guess if I can get home before tomorrow night, get this maid's uniform back and replace my sister's pantyhose, no one will be the wiser as far as I'm concerned."

"Are we all agreed then?" I asked.

Spazz and Debbie nodded. Lauren shrugged. "I wouldn't want to be the party pooper but it beats me what Debbie is gonna say to her dad. Convince him she ran off with Billy T, but the marriage only lasted a weekend, or what?"

"I'll think of something," Debbie said.

I led our group back to the others.

"We've agreed to give you time to get away, but we'd like you to let Debbie phone her dad and tell him she's okay. We'll give you time to get away, and we've also decided to try to see that you stay free. Nobody knows that Lauren, Spazz and I are missing and Debbie will make up some story to try to get you guys off the hook. You'll have to trust us on that."

Glory threw her arms around me and kissed me. Then she hugged the others. Melvin and Nosh were grinning and shaking our hands. Debbie kissed Nosh on the cheek and he beamed from ear to ear.

"Come," Glory said. "We'll take you downstairs."

We had all just stepped out of the elevator onto the ground floor when a voice boomed outside. "This is the police. We have the building surrounded." The voice echoed. "Don't do anything foolish. We want to talk to you."

────── FIFTEEN ──────

"Oh God!" Glory gasped. "It's too late. The cops are here. What will we do?"

"I guess we'd better just give ourselves up," Melvin said. "What else can we do? I hope they won't fire any of that tear gas or anything."

Nosh looked worried and frightened.

"We had a chance to get away and we messed it up," Glory said. "They must have tailed the van when we went for food. But how did they know? We didn't use the van in the first place. You ditched my old car miles from here, didn't you Melvin?"

Melvin nodded.

"Then how did they find us?" Glory sighed.

"I think I know," Debbie said. "I gave my father a clue when I phoned. Remember, I called him Woofie? It's the name on a building near here, A dog food company. I'm sorry. I didn't know you were going to let us go."

"I repeat, this is the police," the voice boomed out again. "The building is surrounded."

Glory grinned bitterly. "What a dummy I am. We've grown up all our lives in this neighbourhood. Of course I know the Woofie building. How could I have not caught on when you told me it was a pet name for your dad? Melvin, you'd better holler out that we're coming out. Tell them not to shoot. Tell them we don't have any weapons."

"Wait," I said. "I've been looking out this window here. I can't see any police around. Shouldn't they have search lights on this place or something? Wait a minute! That building over there. It's all lit up. You can only see part of the wall but there's a lot of light on the bit you can see."

Glory joined me at the window. "That's the Woofie Building," she said. "They must have cops all over the place."

"But don't you see," I said. "I think they've surrounded the wrong building. I think it's the Woofie Building that's surrounded, not this one. You might still have a chance to slip away."

"You think so?" Glory asked. I could hear the hope rise in her voice.

"Where's your van?" I asked.

"It's behind the old pump house along the other side of this building," Melvin said. "We can reach it by a side door."

"But won't the police have road blocks all over the place?" Lauren asked.

"Maybe," Spazz said. "But the Woofie Building is one street over and maybe they're sure we're inside."

"You can't wait any longer," I said. "It's worth a try. If you leave now, you may get through before they cordon off the whole area."

"Wait," Debbie said. "We have to come too."

"What?" Lauren asked. "Why?"

"Because even if Glory and Nosh and Melvin get away, eventually the police will search every building. They'll find us and then how will we explain what we're doing here? Glory and her brothers will be charged with four kidnappings, not one."

"She's right," I said. "It will be hard to concoct a story to satisfy the police with the four of us here. We're wasting time."

"It will turn out the same way, though," Spazz said. "If they stop the van and find the four of us in it."

"Yeah," Debbie said. "But if we get through, it gives them a much better chance of not being arrested, if I'm the only one who has to come up with a story later."

"Send someone out to talk," the voice

boomed again. "We need to talk."

"We're wasting time. Are you willing to chance taking us with you, Glory?" Debbie asked. "You have to decide now."

Glory nodded. She looked at Melvin and Nosh. They nodded too.

"Let's go, Melvin," I said. "Take us to the van."

"Wait," Glory said, "I'm not leaving our instruments behind, no matter what happens."

She grabbed a guitar. Nosh grabbed the keyboard and Melvin the other guitar. "What about the amps?" he asked.

"Leave them," Glory said.

"Spazz and I've got them," I said. "Go on, let's go."

Spazz and I quickly wound up the electrical cords and hefted the two amps. Lauren grabbed a mike and we followed Melvin down a passageway to a door. He pushed it open, looked out, then waved us to follow. It was pitch dark outside and we didn't see the small building that Melvin had called the pumphouse until we were right on top of it. The van was parked behind it.

Melvin slid the side door back and Debbie, Lauren and Glory clambered in. He opened the back door and Spazz and I shoved the amps inside along with the cords and mike. Nosh jumped in the back, Melvin slammed the door and ran around to the driver's side as Spazz and I scrambled onto the front seat.

The van coughed and sputtered when Melvin tried to start it, then with a rumble, the motor caught. It sounded like the muffler was missing.

"Take it slow, Melvin," I said. "We don't want to scream out of here or every cop in the neighbourhood will be after us."

Melvin eased the van forward and into an alleyway that ran behind the building. The alley let us onto a side street and Melvin turned left. I held my breath, I guess everyone was doing the same, waiting for the sound of police sirens. We crossed one intersection and were halfway down the next block when, in front of us, from the middle of the street, a light was directed at us.

Spazz gasped. "It's a cop. Debbie, get down in the back."

"Melvin, be cool," I said. "Don't try anything like flooring it and getting away. There's a police car on the side of the road and another cop standing beside it."

"Let me do the talking," Spazz said. "The cop with the light is on my side of the van. Somebody pass me one of those guitars from the back, quick."

Someone did and Spazz wound down the window as we pulled up beside a cop with a large flashlight.

My heart was pounding. Spazz was going

to do the talking? What, I wondered, could he say that would get us out of this? I hoped he wasn't going to try singing his way out.

"Good evening, folks. Where are you all off to this evening?" The cop shone his flashlight inside the van. I glanced over my shoulder. Debbie was nowhere in sight. In the back, behind Lauren and Glory and surrounded by the amps, sat Nosh, clutching his keyboard.

"We've got a gig," Spazz said. He tapped the guitar he was holding and ran a finger over a couple of strings. "In one of the clubs downtown."

I thought, please don't ask Spazz to play you anything. And what club? I knew I didn't really look old enough to be allowed in any club where they sold liquor. I bet the cop's gonna ask, what club?

"You know you really should have the muffler on this van looked at, it's not only noisy, but the fumes ..." The cop was beginning to choke in the oily smoke from the van's exhaust. He coughed and waved the smoke from around his head. "It's dangerous. I could give you a ticket."

"We'll have it seen to officer," Spazz said. "We've got some money coming in tonight from this gig. We haven't had many lately. Been down on our luck so we can't afford to be late."

"Well, make sure you get it fixed pretty

quick. Your passengers in the back there will be getting their lungs full of carbon monoxide. Better drive with the windows open, okay."

"Okay," Spazz said. "Thanks officer."

"By the way, what's the name of your group?" the cop asked. He started coughing and the van rumbled louder as Melvin shifted his foot on the gas.

"Uh," Spazz mumbled, "um, Kidnapped Cupcake."

I gulped and I was sure I heard Lauren gasp behind me but the cop was spluttering and waving us on.

Melvin put the van in gear and we rumbled forward leaving the cop in a cloud of exhaust fumes.

"Kidnapped Cupcake," I gasped. "Are you crazy or what Spazz? How could you come up with a name like that? You almost gave us away."

"Sorry," Spazz said. "I wasn't prepared for that one. I just said the first name that came into my head. Anyway, I don't think the cop heard me. Melvin was revving the van and the cop was nearly dying from the exhaust fumes."

"Where now?" Melvin asked. "We can't afford to be stopped again."

"Spazz told the cop we have a gig downtown," I said. "You'd better make it look like we're heading that way in case those cops are still watching us."

"Right," Melvin said. "I'll turn left at the next block. It takes us directly to the free-way for downtown."

He was right. As soon as we turned left, we had no other option, other than making a U-turn, than to turn right onto the freeway. A few minutes later, we saw the well-lit skyline of downtown. The blue neon sign on top of The Ritz Plaza stood out in particular.

"Where will we drop you off?" Glory asked. "Debbie has to call her dad. Are you still gonna give us a chance to leave town?"

"Yes," Debbie said. "You could drop us off near a phone booth. Then what are you gonna do?"

"This freeway is heading west, I think we'll just keep on going," Glory said. "We'll go as far as our gas money takes us."

"Hey," Spazz said. "I've got an idea. What time is it anyway?"

"Ten-fifteen," Debbie said.

"Great, it's still early," Spazz said. "This freeway passes just two blocks from The Ritz Plaza. Why don't you drop us off there? Kevin and I still have to collect our money for the job Billy T gave us. We agreed to stick around until Monday anyway."

"You've got to be kidding," I said. "You're not suggesting that we go back inside that hotel are you? There's no way I'm sticking around until Monday anyway, and Lauren has to be home tomorrow too."

"Look," Spazz said. "We agreed to give Glory, Melvin and Nosh some time. We've even agreed to let them get away completely if they can, and Debbie can come up with a good cover story. She's gonna need a bit of time to think. So, what better place than the Royal Suite of The Ritz Plaza? Besides we never did get a chance to use that hot tub. I need to relax and I'd like to collect my money when Billy T gets back."

"You're crazy," I said.

"And what about me?" Lauren asked. "You surely don't expect me to walk in there wearing this maid's outfit."

"Why not?" Spazz asked. "You did before."

Lauren sighed. "I used the back stairs. I doubt if I could get away with that again. And now, without my dark pantyhose on, I'm gonna stick out like a sore thumb."

"I think I have an old coat back here somewhere," Glory said. "You can have it if you like. It's long. It'll cover your uniform."

"Great, that's settled then," Spazz said.

"What is?" I asked.

"Melvin here will drop us off near The Ritz Plaza," Spazz went on. "We'll go in and give Debbie a few minutes to concoct a story. Then she can phone her dad. The girls can go home. You can too, if you want, Kevin. Or you and I can spend the night there. I did say we'd stay until Monday. You even told your mother, remember?"

"Yeah, but that was before all this happened. Anyway, how are we gonna get in again?"

"Let's try it, okay? If we don't get in, Debbie can still find a phone and call her dad and tell him she'll be home shortly. If we're gonna make sure Debbie doesn't get questioned by the police, at least until Glory and her brothers get well outta town, we've gotta hang around somewhere. I'd rather spend the couple of hours in The Ritz Plaza's Royal Suite than hanging around the bus station or someplace like that. Okay with you, Debbie?"

"Yeah. Sounds good."

"We're only a few blocks from the hotel now," Melvin said. "What do you want to do?"

"Take a right at the next turnoff," Spazz said. "You can't stop on this freeway. You can drop us off one street over and we'll walk the rest of the way. Then you can get back on this freeway."

Melvin pulled the van into the right lane and drove up a short ramp to the street that ran parallel to us. He pulled over to the curb and switched off the motor.

We climbed out and Glory got out with the girls. She opened the rear door of the van and Nosh stepped out while she rummaged around for her coat.

"Here it is." She helped Lauren slip it on. It covered her almost to her ankles. "It fits fine," Glory said.

"Thanks," Lauren said. "But I think Spazz's idea is crazy."

Melvin had got out of the van too. He shook our hands. "Thanks, you guys. We really appreciate what you're doin'."

Glory hugged us. "Thanks again. You're really great kids. I'm sorry we messed you around, really sorry." She had tears in her eyes. "Thanks for giving us a second chance."

"Here. Take this," Spazz said. "It's a little extra gas money, courtesy of Billy T. It might get you a bit further."

"Oh you're a sweet kid, Spazz." Glory kissed him on the cheek. "I'll send you all a postcard from California if we make it. Bye."

She climbed into the van beside Melvin. Nosh climbed in, grinning, after Debbie gave him a special hug.

Melvin started the van and we were immediately covered in black smoke.

"Keep on playin', you guys," Spazz called. "You hear?"

We waved as Melvin eased the van away from the curb.

"Oh wait," Glory yelled. "I want to give you this." She passed a cassette tape out the window to Spazz. "It's us. Some of the songs you liked."

Then they were gone. We stood on the sidewalk waiting for the fumes to clear. A block away, the brightly lit entrance of The Ritz Plaza glowed in the darkness.

SIXTEEN

"So how do you figure they're gonna let us in again?" I asked.

Spazz didn't answer. He reached inside his jacket and pulled out the black Billy T wig and pulled it over his hair.

"I didn't know you still had that," I said.

"I kept it as a souvenir. How do I look?" he asked when he had it adjusted.

"Okay, I guess. But after all the stuff that's been in the papers, aren't they gonna freak out when we walk in there?"

"May-be. But if they still think I'm Billy T they may not say anything. I am renting the suite or at least Billy T is, and you saw what they said in the newspaper. The hotel keeps the comings and goings of its guests confidential. Now, you ready to try it or not? How about you two girls?"

"Oh Spazz, you're really weird," Lauren said, laughing. "Why not?"

"Just let me fix this," Debbie said. She tucked a small piece of Spazz's blonde hair under the wig. "Perfect. Now do I walk in there as the new wife of Billy T Banko or just one of your groupies?" She burst out laughing.

"I'm hoping you won't be recognized," Spazz said. "I think we should just walk fast, straight to the elevator, just like we own the place. Come on —"

"Oh. God," I groaned. "Here we go again."

Spazz started walking fast towards the entrance of the hotel. We had to scamper to catch up. When we reached the corner where the girls had been gathered the day before, I was relieved to see it was deserted. I didn't fancy dashing into the hotel with a mob of screaming girls at our heels.

We reached the foot of the steps leading up to the front doors. The doorman was nowhere in sight. I noticed Lauren pulling the collar of Glory's coat up around her face like she was trying to shrink down inside it.

We were close together, scrambling up the steps when I remembered. "Spazz," I called. He was a step ahead of me. "The key! We don't have a room key!"

Spazz paused only briefly, then he was through the doors. The three of us again had to rush to catch up to him. Again, I felt the plush carpeting of the lobby underfoot. There were only a few late diners at the tables as we passed and there was no sign of the orchestra.

Spazz was making a beeline for the elevators and we were hot on his heels. We'd almost reached them when a figure stepped out from behind one of the potted ferns.

"Why, Mr. Banko. You've returned. How nice to see you again."

I nearly died. It was Stanley.

"Thanks," Spazz mumbled.

Stanley pressed an elevator button and one of them opened immediately. We hurried inside and Stanley stepped in after us. He produced his special key again and opened the little box as before.

My heart was pounding. Were we going to get away with it? I couldn't believe Stanley didn't recognize Debbie and why didn't he ask Spazz any questions about what had happened?

The elevator was well on its way to the top floor before he finally spoke. "I'll let security know you've returned, Mr. Banko. I know on behalf of myself and the rest of the security staff, we deeply regret the incident yesterday afternoon. We've had the damage to the door to your suite repaired. You may rest assured it won't happen again."

"That's okay, Stanley," Spazz said. "But

could we keep it quiet, you know, the fact that I'm back?"

"But Mr. Banko... I'm bound to tell the manager and I'm sure he'll want to make every arrangement to see you're not disturbed."

"Well, maybe just between you and me and the manager, okay? The fewer people who know I'm here the better."

"Very good sir, I'll convey your request to the manager."

We'd passed the thirty-fourth floor and then the elevator door was opening.

"Oh Stanley, I completely forgot to take a room key with me with all the excitement," Spazz said.

"Not to worry, sir. I have a master key right here." Stanley held the elevator door open for us. "Will there be anything else, sir?" he asked as he unlocked the door to the suite, stepped inside and switched on the lights.

"No thank you Stanley, that's fine, just fine," Spazz said.

"Very good sir. If you require anything, just pick up the phone." He bowed and closed the door quietly behind us, leaving us alone.

"Am I an actor or am I an actor?" Spazz said, grinning his head off. Debbie and Lauren collapsed on one of the couches, laughing like crazy. Spazz pulled off his jacket and our rope fell to the floor. "Anyone any good at untying knots? I wouldn't mind getting my expensive tie back."

"I suppose there's no hope of salvaging my sister's pantyhose?" Lauren asked.

"'Fraid not. They look just a little out of shape. Next time, Kevin, old boy, when you yank on a girl's pantyhose do it gently."

I hit him on the head with a cushion from one of the easy chairs.

"Debbie, you'd better phone your father and let him know you're okay," I said.

"Okay. Just give me a sec. It has to sound reasonable."

Spazz went off to one of the bedrooms and came back with a swimsuit. "I'm hitting the hot tub," he announced. "There's another guy's pair in there, Kevin, but I'm afraid girls, I couldn't find anything for you. Guess you'll have to skinny dip."

"No way," Lauren said. "Anyway didn't that guy Stanley say if you needed anything to just phone. Surely, Spazz, the great Billy T Banko can conjure up a couple of swimsuits for us girls and, while you're at it, a pair of black pantyhose, medium."

"Okay, okay. Your wish is my command."

"Just a sec," I said. Debbie had picked up the phone. She looked worried as she di- alled. "Daddy. It's me... Yes, I'm fine. Really Daddy... I'm not kidnapped. It was a mistake... Yes, I'm free. Just listen for a sec Daddy. I'm with some friends. It was all a big mix up. I got caught up with a sorority group. They were thinking of asking me to join. They were celebrating and they got carried away. It was just a prank, Daddy. Somebody got carried away... I know it was a bad joke and you must have been worried... I didn't go along with it. The person who did it is really upset... No, I'd rather not give you her name. She's apologized... No, I'm not interested in joining their sorority either.

"The phone call? Um. I don't know where they got our number. Someone just dialled and handed me the phone and some note to read. I thought I was talking to some Eastridge kid, some sort of initiation. No. I wasn't high on drugs or anything. You know I wouldn't do drugs. Trust me, Daddy.

"Woofie? Yeah, a nickname, I think. Look, did you call the police? You did. Oh, dear. Listen Daddy, could you explain to them that I'm okay and it was just a prank. I know they'll take a serious view of it, but Daddy, please, I don't want to get anyone in trouble. Coming home? I'd like to stay a little longer. No I'm not with the sorority group, I left with some friends. Uh, Lauren Malone."

I heard Lauren gasp.

"Okay, I'll put her on. He wants to talk to you." Debbie motioned for Lauren to take the phone. Lauren protested but she took the phone from Debbie anyway.

"Hello, yes, this is Lauren. Yes, Debbie is fine. We're just with a few friends. I'll see that she gets home safely, Mr. Dobrazynski, I promise. Okay." She handed the phone back to Debbie.

"Daddy, don't wait up… Oh, please, I'll be home in a couple of hours… By midnight? But it's ten-thirty now. I'll be home by one, I promise… Oh thanks Daddy, I love you. Bye." Debbie put the phone down and collapsed into a chair.

"He's gonna square it with the police. But I've got to be home by one. I gave him my word."

"You're quite an actress too," Spazz said, grinning. "There's still time for a dip in the hot tub. Let me phone down for the swimsuits and the pantyhose. Then I think I've just got enough of Billy T's cash to send you girls home by cab."

Spazz was getting us some soft drinks from the bar. The girls and I were sitting soaking in the tub. The hotel had come through. Stanley had delivered the swimsuits personally and Lauren was satisfied with the pantyhose. Debbie and Lauren said the swimsuits didn't look too glamorous with Ritz Plaza emblazoned across them, but they looked terrific to me.

"And here's the pop," Spazz announced, as he entered carrying a tray. He grinned. "Or, would anyone care for some Parfait Amour?"

"No way," Lauren said. "Last time I drank that stuff I got kidnapped."

"Holy! That reminds me." I leaped out of the tub.

"Where are you going?" Lauren demanded.

"Just going to put the safety chain on that door."

——— SEVENTEEN ———

When the two phones rang, Spazz and I were just finishing the breakfast that room service had delivered and listening to Glory's tape. We'd played the tape over and over the night before until the girls had taken the cab home and all four of us had agreed it was great.

The phones continued to ring. We looked at each other. Who could be phoning us?

"I guess we'd better answer one of them," Spazz said.

I got up and picked up the nearest phone.

"Hello," I said nervously.

"Hello, Spazz?"

I thought I recognized the voice.

"Uh. No. It's Kevin."

"Oh. Hi Kevin. This is Billy T. I hope I didn't wake you guys up. I'm not sure what time it is there, it's noon here. I'm not good at time zones."

"You didn't wake us," I said. "Spazz is right here."

"Good. Say, if you flip the switch on the phone on the desk there, the two of you can hear me and talk to me. It's a speaker phone."

"I'm using the phone on the desk now," I said. "Just a sec." I found the switch Billy mentioned and flipped it on.

"It's on," I said.

"Good. So how's it going, Spazz?"

"Um. Okay," Spazz replied.

"Say, who's that singing in the background?"

"Oh, it's a friend of ours," Spazz answered. "It's a tape. I'll just turn it down."

"No, don't do that, let me hear some more of it."

"You want me to turn up the volume?" Spazz asked.

"Yeah and take the phone near the stereo off the hook too."

We did that and when the song came to the end, Spazz turned down the volume.

"That's great stuff," Billy said. "Who is that? I've never heard that group before."

"It's a new group," Spazz said. "They haven't been recorded yet. You want to hear one more song?"

"Yeah, sure. Play one more."

Spazz turned up the volume as Glory was just starting to belt out another song.

Billy, Spazz and I listened in silence until that song ended. Then Billy came on the line again.

"Hey, you guys, can you send me a copy of that tape? That group is really fantastic. You say they haven't been recorded?"

"No," Spazz said.

"Well how can I get in touch with them? And who is that woman singing? Great voice. Do you have their phone number or their address?"

"No," I answered. "We don't have any address or phone. They just moved. They're on their way to Los Angeles. They left last night. They're driving."

"I'll be in L.A. at the end of next week. What's the group's name? I'd like to contact them. I'm looking for a band to open my next live performance. Not heavy metal, something in contrast to us. They sound like they might be what I'm looking for. Can you send me a copy by express? I'd like to hear the rest of the tape before I contact them. They have more songs, don't they?"

"Yeah," Spazz said. "This tape has fifteen songs on it. The singer's name is Glory."

"Glory what?"

"Just Glory," Spazz replied. "I don't know her last name. I don't know how you'll track them down."

"So what's the group's name?"

"They don't really have one."

"Spazz nicknamed them Kidnapped Cupcake," I laughed.

"Does that mean something?" Billy asked.

"Not really," Spazz mumbled.

"So send me a copy of the tape. Send it to my L.A. address. Got a pencil?"

I found a pen and some Ritz Plaza letterhead on the desk. "Go ahead," I said.

After Billy had given us his address he continued. "Say, listen. The reason I phoned was to thank you guys and let you know that Vicky and I have decided to stay here a few days longer. We won't be back Monday like we'd planned."

"But ..." Spazz said.

"So I don't want to hold you guys up any longer. You can leave anytime you want. In fact, I'm gonna phone the hotel back and ask them to pack up the few clothes I have there and ship them to me. I don't expect to be back in that city for a while. So if you guys just want to leave today, that's fine. If I send each of you a cheque, will that be okay?"

"Sure," Spazz and I said together.

"Okay give me your addresses."

We did.

"I hope everything went okay. You didn't have any trouble did you?" Billy went on. "I got a weird phone call from my agent."

"Well, our walk around town did attract a few girls," Spazz said. "They kinda mobbed the place. Security had a bit of trouble, but everything's cool now."

"Oh, great. Anyway thanks again. Vicky and I really appreciated you giving us a chance to sneak off. I'll send you the cheques, you send me the tape, okay. Oh, and I'll look after everything as far as the hotel is concerned. See ya guys."

"Wait," Spazz said. "I think we should tell you we bought a couple of ties at Friedbergs. They were kinda expensive. We charged them to your account."

"Forget it. No problem," Billy said. "Oh, that reminds me, Spazz. Do you mind if I keep your jacket? I like it."

"Sure." Spazz laughed.

"You and Kevin can keep the ones you have. Fair exchange. Okay?"

"Great," Spazz said. "And thanks."

Billy hung up.

"Yahoo," Spazz said. "Let's get out of here. I think I've had enough of life at The Ritz, how about you?"

"Yeah. Let's go. We'll even be home a day early."

"I'm afraid we'll have to take the bus. Sorry, but I gave Debbie and Lauren the last of my money for the cab. It's back to being plain old

Spazz again. I guess I won't be needing this anymore." He tossed the Billy T Banko wig onto a couch. "Let's take the back stairs," he said as we slipped out the door of The Ritz Plaza's Royal Suite.

EIGHTEEN

It's been nearly two months now since what Spazz and I call our 'Weekend at The Ritz.'

Our cheques arrived from Billy T just a few days after his phone call. Spazz has spent most of his money already on new clothes. He's given up buying at The Thrift Shop. The clothes there just don't fit his new image since he started dating Debbie Dobrazynski. Lauren and I are still going together too.

Debbie's dad was able to smooth things over with the police and Debbie hinted that a big donation to the Police Benefit Fund didn't hurt. Her dad wasn't convinced that she should continue at Eastridge High, until Debbie told him that the sorority girls who pulled the kidnapping prank were all from a private school.

Debbie did have to suffer through a lot of

stares and questions at school when she went back that Monday, but she kept her cool and ignored most of them. The rumour went round that it must have been some kind of publicity stunt on the part of Billy T's agent.

A postcard came for all four of us yesterday. It was addressed to us at the school and it was from Glory. It had been mailed from L. A.

Here's what Glory said: "Sorry for taking so long to send this, but we were lying low for a while. Guess what? Tomorrow night we're the opening act at Black Vulture's live concert at Hollywood Bowl. Can you believe it? And it's all thanks to you. Billy T was looking for us for over six weeks and he found us only because he put an ad in 'The Los Angeles Times'. I saw the ad. It asked that 'Glory and Kidnapped Cupcake' phone a certain number about a recording contract. We're going to be making our first record next week in one of those fancy recording studios we always dreamed about. Billy T suggested we change our name but I said no. Spazz gave it to us and Nosh really loves it. Wish us luck. Love from Glory, Nosh and Melvin."

One last thing — the other day my dad was searching through his closet and he finally asked Mom if she'd seen his favourite sports coat.

"You mean, that old green corduroy thing with the patches on the sleeves?"

"Yeah my favourite. Where is it?"

"I thought you didn't wear it anymore. I gave it to The Thrift Shop a couple of months ago. Even that crazy friend of Kevin's, Spazz what's-his-name, wouldn't be seen dead in that. And you know how he dresses when he's pretending to be some rock singer like Green Rooster or whatever they call themselves."

Then I remembered where I'd seen Spazz's jacket before. If Mom only knew.

—— About the Author ——

Frank O'Keeffe lives on a farm near Edson, Alberta where he raises cattle. He is also a substitute teacher, writer, storyteller and in his spare time he presents writing workshops for children.

One of his sons liked to listen to heavy metal and when he left high school, he went to Vancouver with some friends to form a band. They weren't as successful as Black Vulture, but they still had a lot of fun. Now that same son hopes to become a famous chef in a hotel just like The Ritz Plaza.